Clarissa Ross

GEMINI IN DARKNESS

MAGNUM EDITIONS

MAGNUM BOOKS
NEW YORK

GEMINI IN DARKNESS

PRESTIGE BOOKS INC. • 18 EAST 41ST STREET
NEW YORK, N.Y. 10017

HOUSE OF
DARK SIGNS

"You see Madam Helene merely as an ailing old woman who has lived beyond her time, an astrologer and no more," Dr. Gill said narrowly. "She is more than that. She has a genius for ESP. She communes with spirits. Madam Helene is unique; rarely does her sort appear on earth."

Diana heard him out, fascinated by his oratory, by the shrewd eyes that glittered wildly as he spoke of the woman residing upstairs as if she were a witch! She could not resist deflating him. "But Madam Helene is human," she said softly. "She will certainly die one day soon. What then?"

Dr. Gill's voice grew strange. He stared at Diana. "The harvest of Madam Helene's genius will never be lost. We will find someone under her favored sign to replace her, someone whose talents can be developed. Our mission will go on—it *must* . . ."

With those eyes on her face, Diana felt a sudden chill go through her.

CHAPTER ONE

The first time Diane Lewis saw the house on Beacon Street was on a humid, hot night in August. For almost two weeks there had been this sickening heat and Diana along with the other residents of Boston had been suffering under it. Even the boon of air-conditioning in most public rooms, offices and other gathering places did not help much. Many apartments had just window units for bedrooms and these offered only a partial release from the stifling, continuing heat. In Diana's case such a unit had been no use at all since it had broken down almost at the moment the heat wave began and the landlord of the building in which she had the tiny apartment was conveniently off to Cape Cod for a vacation complete with ocean breeze.

In a way this was only one of the signs. And later, when she was to look back on those days, she would recognize that there had been a number of portents along the way, misadventures that had been inevitably pointing to some momentous climax. But as she stood hesitantly on the sidewalk at dusk and stared up at the majestic red brick building with its ornate trim

5

of gray stone and its worn stone steps with black iron railings she little dreamed what awaited her behind its heavy oaken entrance door.

Standing there in the gathering shadows of the humid night she briefly debated whether to keep the appointment she had made or not. Some warning inner voice told her to go back. Retreat to nearby Arlington Street and the Public Gardens from which she'd just come. Take the Arlington Subway back to Brookline and the sickening heat of her apartment. It was the thought of returning to that heat again which convinced her and made her mount the worn steps to press the button of the unmarked bell. And so she'd taken the first step into a nightmare!

Diana's wildest imaginings could not have matched what she would experience in the weeks that followed. It had all begun simply enough—simply, but not too simply—for the classified ad she was now answering had contained one item of information that had irresistibly captured her fancy.

The ad, for a female secretary, had appeared in the staid *Boston Globe*. Diana had been going through the various job offerings when she came on this one that caught her attention:

"PERSONAL SECRETARY, for unique confidential post of prime importance. Applicant should have degree, typing and shorthand, be of pleasing personality and have been born approximately five minutes before midnight on May 23. Write to box G7710."

She'd been sitting in her tiny kitchenette sipping iced coffee with the paper spread out on the table. She

6

read and then reread the item with a surprised smile crossing her attractive, oval face. The thing that amused her was that she'd actually been born on May 23, 1945 and her mother had more than once mentioned that her exact birth time had been five minutes before midnight.

Diana was only wearing a mini-kimono of yellow terrycloth belted at the waist, as she was just finishing breakfast preparatory to taking a shower and braving the Boston heat to go job hunting. Her brown, wavy hair which she wore at shoulder length was now tied back in a ponytail, and her large intelligent eyes twinkled as she rose from the table.

A glance at her wristwatch told her Adam Purcell, whom she'd been dating steadily for almost six months, would be at his office. He worked for a public relations firm which had its headquarters on St. James Street; however, he was out of town a good deal. This happened to be one of the weeks when he would be remaining in the city. She hastily tore the advertisement out of the paper and went to the phone in the living room to dial his number.

Seating herself on the arm of the worn divan that came with the furnished apartment, she waited to be connected to his office. A smile brightened her pleasantly freckled face and there was a roguish look in her brown eyes which were her best feature. She was anticipating the reaction of Adam and expecting it to be emphatic. Adam was a nice young man, but he had just a hint of sedate Boston about him. Since she was from upper New York State she felt free to tease him about Boston propriety.

7

He came on the line, "Adam Purcell here."

She laughed. "Diana most decidedly here!"

"Oh, it's you," he said in a more casual tone. "I wasn't expecting to hear from you until this evening."

"I know," she said. "But something really weird and maybe wonderful has come up. I think I have a good job offer if I want it."

"Great!" Adam said happily. He'd been worried that she would have to leave town and break up their romance. "Is it from another publishing house?"

"No," she said. She might have expected him to jump to that conclusion. She'd been working for a regional monthly and doing well. Unfortunately a quarrel with the editor had left her without a job or a recommendation. She told Adam, "It's not likely I'll get another magazine offer in Boston. There aren't that many magazines published here. That's why this looks so good."

Adam sounded sort of impatient as he said, "You haven't told me yet what it is."

"It's a way-out kind of thing, but just right for me," she said. And she proceeded to read him the advertisement. She wound up with, "I was born at that time and on that date. I'm a Gemini. Whoever wants a secretary must be hipped on the subject of astrology."

"I don't like the sound of it at all," Adam's tone was pained.

"I was afraid of that," she admitted with a sigh. "But if I don't get a job soon I'll have to go back to New York. I can't live here without working."

8

"I know," he said. "But a job is bound to come along."

"Not on a magazine," she argued. "It's practically a hundred and ten in the shade in this apartment with the air-conditioner not working. If I don't get a job in a nice, cool office soon I'll probably die of heat prostration."

"I'm sorry," he said.

"It's easy to be sympathetic in a nice cool office. I'm going to answer that box number and maybe I'll wind up in an air-conditioned suite too."

"Diana, I can't talk long now. I've got a conference coming up in a couple of minutes. But don't answer that thing until we discuss it. I'd say it's probably some kook stunt to sell something. It can't be on the level!"

Her pert face shadowed with annoyance. "Of course it can," she said into the phone. "And I'm practically certain to be the only one with the qualification for the job. How many available girl secretaries here in Boston were born on May 23 at five minutes to twelve?"

"Hundreds I hope," he said unhappily. "Don't do anything. I'll talk to you when I see you tonight."

Diana put the phone down with a bleak look. She studied the torn-out item again and went over to her writing desk. She selected a sheet of her personal notepaper and began writing a reply to the advertisement. When she went out an hour later she dropped the letter into the nearest mailbox. Adam could protest all he liked, she was going to find out what the classified had to offer. If the job seemed even fair she was going to take it; she needed the money.

Adam and she had a date for the Boston Pops' outdoor concert on the bank of the Charles River. Arthur Fiedler's conducting was treasured by both of them and they often attended these pop symphony specials. But with the argument about her applying for the weirdly-advertised post they found themselves in no mood for listening to the concert. They needed to use all their time to talk it out.

So they wound up in the cocktail lounge atop the Prudential Tower. There, high above the twinkling lights and blatant neon of the old city, they sat facing each other at a table near a window. The light was properly subdued and in the background a jazz trio ground out their versions of popular songs of the summer.

Diana sipped her Tom Collins. "The drink is cool and so is the lounge. What a change from my apartment!"

He frowned over his martini. "It says there'll be rain tomorrow."

"Thunder showers," she corrected him. "Hot thunder showers. Don't build up my hopes for nothing."

He stared at her, his even-featured face sternly handsome in the shadows of the lounge. In stark daylight he didn't look quite that well. He had mottled skin, not bad but noticeable, the result of a severe acne in boyhood. And his hair, which merely looked blond in this dim light, had a dry, straw tone. Yet all in all he was a neat-appearing young executive.

He said, "Why did you send that letter to the *Globe* when I asked you not to?"

"I thought I should," she told him. "Since Elsie left to get married I've been paying the full rent for the

10

apartment. And don't suggest I get another girl to take her place in sharing it with me; I've had enough of that. In this heat I'm not up to screening dim possibilities. I'd rather go on paying the rent alone, if I find a decent job."

"You want it all your way."

"You're not being fair," she chided him. "I could easily find a job in New York. I only want to remain in Boston because of us. Or is that important to you?"

Adam winced. "You know it is."

"Well, then," she said. "You never hear me complain. And I could. Lately your firm has kept you out of town more than you're in."

"I'm here all this week."

"And we're having a heat wave," she said with a grimace.

Adam cleared his throat. She recognized this as a familiar part of his build-up whenever he tried to convince her he was being extremely fair and reasonable. He said, "I want what is best for you, Diana. But I don't like the sound of this job. It's either some kind of stunt or whoever put it in the paper is unbalanced. Either way it's no good."

"Wait until we see if I get an answer," she suggested.

He stared at her moodily. "I'd be a lot happier if you'd tell me right this minute you wouldn't pay any attention to whatever answer comes."

"I can't do that."

"You know what a crazy world we live in," he worried. "What a way-out town this is for that matter. The Common is creeping with hippies, LSD and mari-

11

juana—you name it. We've got unsolved murders galore, mostly pretty girls like you, and yet you want to expose yourself to some lunatic."

She gave him a patient smile. "I appreciate your concern but you're being silly. I'm positive the advertisement was placed in the paper by a solid business man type. There are plenty of big business people, movie stars and politicians who believe in astrology."

"I haven't met any of them," Adam said.

"That proves exactly nothing," Diana told him. "Wait and see what reply I get."

"It seems to me you're anxious to put yourself in a bad spot," Adam gloomily predicted.

Their evening ended on this note of argument. Even when he kissed her goodnight Adam was somewhat aloof. She let herself into her unpleasantly warm apartment with a feeling of let-down. The furniture and everything about the small rented place seemed shabbier than usual. She faced another night of restless sleep with a feeling of hopelessness. Adam wasn't very considerate it seemed to her. He didn't understand.

Next day there was a violent thunder storm around the noon hour. Diana remained in the apartment and watched the lightning, shivered at the thunder and saw the rain come pouring down. But when it ended and the sun came out, once more it was just as hot. There seemed to be no respite from the heat.

It was around a quarter past three when her phone rang. She picked it up to hear a strange, crisp female voice at the other end of the line. The voice said, "Miss Lewis? Miss Diana Lewis?"

"Yes."

"Are you the young lady who replied to an advertisement in the *Globe?*"

"Yes." She was trying to gather an impression from the woman's voice. She sounded promising. Businesslike and alert. The job might turn out to be really worthwhile.

"One moment, please," the female voice said, "I'll switch you to Dr. Martin Gill."

"Thank you," she said. And she at once began trying to remember if she'd heard the name before. Dr. Martin Gill! It had a familiar ring. And yet she couldn't place it. Would he be a medical doctor, or perhaps a dentist, or even a professor at one of the several Boston colleges? In any event he was a professional of some type and looking for a private secretary.

"Miss Lewis?" the query was put to her by a smooth, unctuous voice.

"Speaking," she said.

"Excellent," came the bland reply over the line. "I have your letter here and I'm much impressed. Geminis are usually intellectuals. And I may say that your rising sign is excellent as well. I mean the exact minute of your birth."

"I'm glad to know it," she said faintly, there could be no doubt of his fanatic interest in astrology.

"Have you ever had your horoscope cast, Miss Lewis?"

"No," she said. "I've always felt I'd like to."

"You must," he said. "I'll see to it that you have a complete horoscope at the earliest moment. But you have written about astrology, haven't you? I read your

13

fine article in a back issue of the magazine which employed you."

This praise pleased Diana. She smiled into the phone. "I had to do a lot of research. And I depended mostly on experts whom I met. But I'm glad you liked it."

"I did, indeed," the man at the other end of the line assured her. "I also noted the picture of you at the rear of the magazine with a short history of your writing career. I feel you are ideally suited to our work."

"What is your work?" she asked.

"I'll explain that when we meet," he said, avoiding a direct answer to her question. "And you familiar with Beacon Street?"

"I know it well."

"Well, our house is at the corner of Arlington and Beacon," he said. "A rather unique location. We have an excellent view of the Public Gardens from the front windows and a fine panorama of the Charles River from the back."

"It sounds delightful," she said. She was picturing the rows of nice old buildings along the famous street. If this Dr. Martin Gill owned and occupied one of them he was likely a wealthy man.

"I think it is," Dr. Martin Gill agreed. And he gave her the number of the mansion. "I'll be working late this evening. Why don't you drop by around nine-thirty?"

"I can come earlier if you like," Diana pointed out.

"No. That will be excellent for me," the man with the unctuous voice said.

"I'll be there," she promised.

14

"I look forward to an interesting conversation with you," Dr. Martin Gill said. "And I hope I can persuade you to join our organization."

Their conversation ended. Diana was fascinated at the prospect of the interview and anxious to learn something about the doctor. She had a friend employed with the *Herald-Traveller* in the social notes department and on an impulse decided to call her. The girl's name was Jennifer Haines and she'd been employed by the same magazine for a few months. Diana looked up the number and dialed it.

When Jennifer came on the line her first reaction was one of pleasure. She was a big blonde girl with a warm manner. "Great to hear from you again, Diana. How are things at the magazine?"

"I'm not there anymore. Trouble with your old friend the editor."

"Him!" Jennifer said with disgust. "Don't talk to me about him! What a creep! I couldn't stay there."

Diana said, "The point is I'm looking for a new job. And I think I have one lined up. But the party interested in hiring me is being very mysterious. I hoped you might be able to find out something about him for me."

"I can try," Jennifer promised.

"His name is Dr. Martin Gill and he has a house on Beacon Street. And he's head of some sort of organization."

"Give me a half-hour," Jennifer said. "I'll phone you back."

The return call came before the half-hour was up.

Jennifer sounded a little uncertain. "I'm afraid I haven't been able to come up with too much."

"Oh?" Diana was disappointed.

"I did find a few things out about this Dr. Gill," her friend went on quickly. "But the information isn't as definite as we like on a newspaper. The organization he's connected with is an astrological publishing service. Maybe you've heard of Madame Helene, the astrologist and prophet? Her name was in the headlines about a year ago when the Governor of Ohio was shot and killed by an insane ex-employee of the state welfare service. Madame Helene had made a prediction weeks before that something like this could happen to the governor. It caused quite a stir."

Diana frowned. "Of course I remember. There were articles about it in all the newspapers and magazines. This Madame Helene is a recluse, a mysterious figure supposed to be very old."

"That's the one," Jennifer agreed. "She makes her chief income through the sale of a monthly magazine and charts which are sold in drugstores and five-and-dimes as well as through the mail."

"I've seen her astrological booklets on the stands," Diana recalled.

"There is a profile study of her in solid black on all of them," her friend said. "Sort of a silhouette. But as far as I can tell there has never been a photogragh of her published. You can't tell from the illustration on the booklets how old she is."

"They probably want me to work on the magazine," Diana said. "I wrote an article on astrology a few months ago and Dr. Gill mentioned seeing it."

"You're right. Dr. Gill happens to be managing Madame Helene's affairs and is also the editor of the magazine. Information on him is fairly vague except that he once lived and practiced in Los Angeles. He apparently has a medical degree but our files aren't complete on that either. That's what I mean when I say the information is pretty vague."

"I guess I needn't worry about it," she said. "He sounded very nice and it is a national company."

There was a brief second of silence from the other end of the phone. Then Jennifer said, "I suppose it's all right if you can adjust to working for an outfit like that. I mean dealing in predictions and so forth. I understand that Madame Helene has private clients as well, for these she works out regular detailed horoscopes. According to the news clippings there are some movie stars and even business men who won't make a move without her advice."

Diana gave a small laugh. "Sounds as if the Madame wields a powerful influence."

"You'd be surprised how powerful," the girl at the other end of the line said dryly. "Once people became deeply involved in a subject such as astrology it can develop into an obsession. Her booklets and charts sell in the millions."

"I think it might be fun working for the company."

"I wouldn't know," Jennifer said. "You'll find yourself on the other side of the counter. Instead of reporting objectively on the prophecies of the stars you'll be merchandising them."

Diana was puzzled by her friend's tone. "You're not

17

suggesting there is anything dishonest about their operation?"

"No. But I don't think it would be for me. Too much spooky stuff. If you should decide to join them don't let them brainwash you."

"I don't imagine they could."

"It's happened before," her friend warned. "Just be on your guard."

Diana put down the phone in a rather puzzled state of mind. While Jennifer had cleared up a lot of the mystery surrounding Dr. Martin Gill she'd also created some by her reluctant endorsement of his efforts as being honest. Diana had never heard his name mentioned in connection with Madame Helene. No doubt he purposely kept well in the background.

But she had read a good deal about the astrologist and her predictions. In all the pieces she'd noticed Madame Helene had been mentioned as being extremely old. The press had played up her predictions more than they had her astrological powers. In many cases they had compared her to Jean Dixon. Along with Miss Dixon the Madame had made predictions about the assassination of President Kennedy and later Martin Luther King. The seer had also made numerous other less sensational prophecies which had come true.

Diana had enjoyed the limited amount of research she'd put into her general article on astrology and felt she might like delving into it more thoroughly. The idea of working on Madame Helene's magazine appealed to her. She was determined to keep her appointment with Dr. Martin Gill even though it would mean breaking a date she had with Adam.

She spent most of the balance of the afternoon rummaging through her papers to find the notes on her article and a couple of cheap reference books she'd purchased at the time of writing it. She was deeply immersed in these when the telephone rang. It was Adam wanting to know what time to drop by for her.

"I can't see you tonight," she explained. "I have a job interview."

"You received an answer?" Adam asked, concerned.

"Yes. From a Dr. Gill on Beacon Street. Is that respectable enough for you?"

"I don't know," he said. "Tell me more."

"I'm seeing him tonight at half-past nine after he finishes at his office. He manages the affairs of Madame Helene, the astrologist."

"That fake prophet!" Adam said with annoyance.

"I don't believe she can be a fake," Diana said at once, defending her prospective employer. "Some of the things she's predicted have happened."

"Sheer luck!" Adam scoffed.

"Maybe. But they want to talk to me about a position on their magazine and I'd like to try it."

"I wish you'd forget all about it," he worried. And then he asked, "Can I go along with you?"

"That would make a dreadful impression," she said. "This is something I have to do on my own. We can get together another time."

He sighed from the other end of the line. "Just be careful, Diana. You don't know what sort of person this Dr. Martin Gill is."

"He must be all right," she said. "I'll phone you in the morning."

Adam hadn't exactly been pleased but she'd won her argument with him. And now on this hot night following an equally hot day she stood on the worn stone steps of the house on Beacon Street waiting for the doorbell to be answered. She was wearing a trim white linen dress whose only decoration was a black shiny belt and a railbow-hued silk handkerchief knotted at her throat. She'd taken some trouble with her long brown hair and it flowed neatly about her shoulders as she waited there feeling more than a little on edge.

Then the heavy oaken door swung open to reveal a prim woman in a plain dark dress standing there. The woman had gaunt, bony features and iron-gray hair. She observed Diana with a slight frown.

"Are you Miss Lewis?" she asked. It was the same crisp female voice Diana had heard on the phone.

"Yes, I'm expected," she said.

"I know," the woman said. She stood back in the shadowed hallway. "You can come in and I'll take you to Dr. Gill."

Diana stepped inside and was at once impressed by the cooler air. As the door was closed behind her, she said, "How pleasant it is in here compared to the street. Do you have central air-conditioning?"

"Some sections of the building," the woman said in her unsmiling way. "We don't actually need it. The walls of these old houses are thick and protect one from the changes in weather."

"So it would seem," she agreed. The ceiling of the hallway was somewhere lost in a shadowy height. The

20

hall was too dark for her to make out where it went. Everything here was ancient and vast and smelling of the dusty bygone days. A kind of pungent odor of age and unidentifiable spice penetrated her nostrils.

"Follow me, please," the woman said. She behaved like a well-regulated automaton. Diana judged her as efficient, but without imagination. The woman spoke again as they walked down the interminable dark hall to the rear of the old building. "I'm usually gone by this time. But I've been working late most evenings as we're short of staff."

"That does make it awkward," Diana agreed, wondering if she liked the atmosphere of the place well enough to work there. Something in the air troubled her. A something she could not at once place. But she decided she was being too critical—an attitude inspired by Adam's antagonistic attitude towards this project.

They passed the door of what was obviously an old-fashioned elevator. It had a solid metal door with a small window of glass three-quarters up it. Behind the glass she could see a dim light which revealed a brick wall in the rear and vibrating cables. The elevator was on its way upstairs as a lighted red button marked, "In Use," clearly indicated.

Noting her interest in the elevator, the woman in black said, "It's ancient but works well. We use it constantly as Madame Helene has her apartment on the top floor."

"I see," Diana said.

At the very end of the hall there was another passage way to make a T formation. This passage ap-

21

parently ran from one side of the building to the other. They turned right and came to an open door on the left. The woman stood by to show Diana into it.

"This is Dr. Gill's office," she said. "He's upstairs with the Madame at the moment. But he'll be down right away. I'm Miss Carlton; I'm in the front office during the day and look after the switchboard."

"Thank you, Miss Carlton," Diana spoke with a polite smile. She was trying to take in the doctor's office and make what she could of it. The room was dimly lighted by a single desk lamp on a rather high stand over the doctor's desk. One end of the room held a number of steel filing cabinets. The other a table on which were neatly set out a series of astrological charts and booklets showing the familiar attractive silhouette of Madame Helene. And on the wall next to the table was the door of a large wall safe of dark gray steel. There were two windows in the rear wall overlooking the Charles River. She could see the moving lights of autos along the expressway running parallel to the river and the distant neon of industrial plants on the other shore.

But what caught her attention and fascinated her more than anything else were the signed portraits of long-ago film stars tacked all over the brown walls of the office. A glance indicated typical fan photos of Jean Harlow, Carole Lombard, Nancy Carroll, Milton Sills, Jack Pickford, Reneé Adoreé and many others she didn't take time to note.

Turning from the photos to speak to Miss Carlton she was mildly astonished to discover the grim, gray-haired woman had vanished in a spectral silence. It struck her as odd but she recalled the woman had spoken of being kept later than usual. No doubt she was anxious to be on her way.

To fill in her time she moved across to closely inspect the lovely features of the glamorous Jean Harlow. She was doing this and speculating on the date of the star's death when she was suddenly aware of a soft footstep behind her. Expecting to see Dr. Martin Gill she wheeled around quickly. But instead she was confronted by a massive swarthy woman with mad, glittering eyes and unkept oily hair. The woman wore a sack-like black dress and one of her hands was thrust towards her. In the palm of the coarse hand there lay a disgusting thing which Diana saw as a rumpled mess of tiny feathers at first. Then she recognized it as the severed head of a chicken with its blood trailing out onto the monstrous woman's dirty palm. With a cry of fear and surprise Diana took a quick step back.

CHAPTER TWO

The terrifying woman grinned at her in an evil fashion and made some guttural sounds. Diana was transfixed with horror at the revolting thing the mad creature held out before her and the general appearance she presented. The gloomy confines of the office had taken on an atmosphere of the unreal.

"Anna!" the name was called out sharply from someone in the shadows of the hall. And in the next moment a tall, impressive-looking man with a hawk face and a domed bald head fringed with graying hair came striding into the room to eye the swarthy woman angrily.

The monster of a woman gasped and a frightened expression crossed the broad, olive-skinned face with its prominent, hairy mole at the lower left of her mouth. Her hand closed on the pitiful severed chicken's head and she turned and waddled out of the room.

The hawk-faced man, immaculate in a light blue business suit and matching shirt and tie, turned to Diana with an apologetic look on his lined, stern face. "This is a most embarrassing situation," he said. And it was the same voice she'd heard on the phone. "I hope Anna didn't scare you out of your wits?"

Diana sighed. "It's all right," she said faintly. "She came on me without warning. And there was that thing in her hand!"

"I know," the man said in an annoyed voice. "She's more than a little demented. She understands English and speaks it haltingly but she's not friendly to strangers. Madame Helene found her in Italy years ago and hired her as a personal maid. She's very devoted to Madame but I'm afraid that's all that can be said for her. I've suggested she be discharged many times but Madame won't hear of it."

"I see," she said, still upset.

"She has a primitive peasant belief in black magic. No doubt that disgusting thing she was holding before you was some test to determine whether you were a danger to the household or not."

Diana managed a wry smile. "I hope that I passed it."

He frowned. "It's no joking matter and Madame Helene shall be told about it. May I introduce myself, I'm Martin Gill and of course you are Diana Lewis."

She shook hands with him and was struck by the strength of his grip. For an older man he seemed extremely alert and in excellent physical shape. There was no suggestion of middle-aged bulge or any of the other aspects of aging other than his baldness.

She said, "I'm very interested in your office. All these photos of movie stars. And they each have personal signatures. You must have known everyone in Hollywood."

25

The hawk face showed a thin smile. "I did know all the big stars of an earlier era. But that was years ago when I practiced out there. Few of them are still living today. They were part of another and, if I may say so, more pleasing and glamorous world."

"I can't blame you for feeling that way."

"It would be hard for someone as young as you to understand," Dr. Martin Gill said. "But I won't bore you with my nostalgia. We have a number of the new stars on Madame Helene's advisory list today. So I still do have some contact with Hollywood."

"I glanced at the charts and booklets on the table," she said.

He smiled and went over to the table and picked up one of the booklets. "I think they are very well put together," he said. "I take the credit for that. Madame supplies the material and I take care of the layout." He passed an opened booklet to her. "I'm assuming that you know our business is the selling of astrological information in various forms."

Diana nodded. "Yes. I did find that out. I suppose nearly everyone has heard of Madame Helene and her prophecies."

The sharp eyes under the bushy gray brows of Dr. Martin Gill fixed on her in almost a hypnotic fashion. He indicated a nearby chair. "Please, sit down." And when she did, he continued, "I'm pleased that you think so well of Madame Helene. She may not be as highly regarded as a prophet as Jean Dixon, but she is the leader in the field of astrology. And she was greatly impressed by your article which I brought to her attention."

"Thank you," she said. She was fascinated by the energy of the tall man. At this fairly late hour in the evening he seemed to radiate enthusiasm and strength. His personality dominated the gloomy surroundings to make them less depressing.

His eyes fairly bored into her as he said, "It may come as a shock to you but we've known for some time that you would be arriving here to join us."

She was startled enough to say, "Isn't that prediction premature since I haven't decided about the position as yet?"

Dr. Martin Gill smiled in his assured fashion. "I have no doubt that you will make up your mind in our favor. And I think editing our magazine might be a rewarding experience for you."

"Is that what you'd want me to do?"

"Yes," the tall man said, walking around behind his desk and carefully seating himself so the reflection from the lamp highlighted his hawk face. "You would be working in close association with me and Madame Helene but you wouldn't be required to correlate your activities with the other branch of our publishing program. The charts and booklets are prepared and mailed out by a staff located in the upper floors of a Washington Street building. Except for my liaison with them they work on their own."

"It sounds like a challenge," she said, beginning to feel the job might turn out to be all that she'd hoped.

The doctor was leaning forward in his chair. "I have been with Madame Helene for some time now. I can promise you she is pleasant to work for. With her advancing age I have gradually assumed more and more

27

of the obligation for the operation of her astrological empire. A great responsibility as I'm sure you'll agree."

"She has made some startling prophecies," Diana said. "And she must have millions of followers."

"Her world total is startling," he agreed with a solemn look on his face. "I'm not at liberty to reveal the exact number. But I hope you won't be skeptical when I tell you that from her apartment on the top floor of this old house she sways the opinion of as many people as do many of the foremost political leaders of this day. In her own fashion the Madame wields a tremendous power."

His voice had risen towards the end of this speech and again she was not only struck by his vitality, but also a little frightened by the obvious light of fanaticism which had appeared in his sharp blue eyes.

She said, "How often is this magazine published?"

"Bi-monthly," he said at once. "It is not the most important of our mediums but it has its place. Madame stresses the charts and booklets, along with her predictions for the press and her personal charts prepared almost daily for prominent clients who have linked their destinies with the stars."

She saw that he was extremely facile in his explanations of the work. There was no question of his dedication. But the weird atmosphere of it all began to make her realize what her friend Jennifer had meant. Could she line herself up with such an operation? Was her belief in the stars sincere enough for her to work with the same dedication of the others? It seemed doubtful.

Almost as if he'd read her mind Dr. Martin Gill

spoke again, "We won't expect you to see things with our eyes until you have learned more of what we are accomplishing here."

She smiled shyly. "I'm not positive that I will ever have your firm belief in the science of astrology."

He showed no upset at this frank statement from her. "There was a time when I scoffed at the mysteries of the zodiac, when I was ignorant of the way the stars rule our destiny. But Madame Helene soon showed me my error. I gave up my successful Hollywood practice and joined her in her work; I have never regretted it."

"There are many people who are skeptical," she said. "I remember I had a number of letters when I wrote my magazine article. Some of the readers felt I was too prejudiced in favor of astrology."

The hawk face of the middle-aged Martin Gill registered approval. "I sensed that in the article myself. And that is how I first became interested in you."

Diana was confused. "But I don't understand. Surely my replying to your advertisement and happening to have been born at exactly five minutes before midnight on May 23 had to be a coincidence. You couldn't have known that I would be answering that advertisement. Or that I had been born at that moment."

He smiled in his mysterious way. "We didn't have to know those things. Madame Helene used her talents to project herself into your future. And she saw your path was going to cross ours. When you replied to my advertisement I was not startled. I recognized your name and realized the prophecy of the Madame had been fulfilled. She claimed you would get in touch with us."

Her eyebrows raised. "But how could she possibly know?"

Dr. Martin Gill shrugged. "I can't explain that. All I can tell you is that she asked me to insert the advertisement and use the date and moment of her own birth. You see she is a Gemini like you. And she was convinced that your birth time would match hers."

"I find this all very strange," Diana said in a bewildered tone. As she was beginning to feel uneasy in the tense atmosphere of the shadowed room.

Once again the immaculately dressed medical man proved himself adept at handling a difficult situation. He got up from behind the desk and came slowly around to stand before her with a smile on his lined, hawk face.

"Of course you find our beliefs strange," he acknowledged in a most genial way. "I only ask you to have a little patience. In the first place you mustn't confuse the Madame's predictions with astrological forecasts alone. There is ESP involved. Madame Helene has developed her powers of extra-sensory perception to a remarkable degree. She can read minds even at a great distance."

"And that is a totally different field."

"Granted," Dr. Martin Gill agreed. "And it is what sets Madame Helene apart from her competitors." Abruptly changing the subject he asked, "Where do you live in Boston?"

"In Brookline," she said. "I have a small apartment."

"Do you have a long lease on it?"

Again she was puzzled. "No. My year is almost up and I haven't renewed. My landlord isn't very good at keeping the place in repair. Just now the air-conditioning isn't working. I did have a girl friend sharing it with me but she left to get married."

The man with the domed bald head and shrewd eyes looked pleased at hearing this. "Then I take it you are not satisfied with your quarters and wouldn't mind changing them?"

"Not at all." She couldn't imagine why this was of any concern of his.

"That fits in with things nicely," Dr. Martin Gill said. "We have an apartment in the house here, air-conditioned by the way, which goes with the job we're offering you."

Once again she was startled. "It's an extremely generous offer," she said.

"Not really," he told her. "Because of Madame Helene's advanced age and the fact I have to make the best use of every minute, it is much more convenient to have the person editing the magazine living in the house."

Diana was wary of the proposition. She recalled the warnings she'd had and worried that she would be too completely under the domination of the strange group operating the astrological service. She said, "I wouldn't have much time to myself."

"As much as you like," he said. "The apartment has its own entrance on the second floor. It is completely self-contained and you'd be independent from the rest of the house. You could go and come as you liked."

31

It sounded almost too good to be true. "I see," she said, sure there must be a catch in it. "And what is the salary?"

He told her what her weekly stipend would be and it was generous. With the free apartment taken into consideration it was more than that. She said, "I have no furniture of my own to move here. My apartment is furnished."

"So is this one," he assured her.

"Who was the former editor?" She inquired, wondering how such an excellent position came to be open.

The hawk-faced doctor at once looked sad. "His name was Walter Glendon. Madame Helene and I were impressed with his talents. I regarded him almost as a son. Unfortunately he had a fatal accident."

"I'm so sorry," she said.

"One of life's little ironies," Dr. Martin Gill said with a deep sigh. "I'm sure he would have had a great future with us. But his life was cut short."

Diana was carefully considering everything. In many ways the position was perfect for her—the free apartment so near the center of the city made it especially attractive. But to counter-balance this she was sure Adam would object to her taking the job at all. And there was a strange something about the house and even this immaculately dressed, glib, older man which made her hesitate. Perhaps it was because the house and the doctor were part of the weird business of prophecy. It seemed a small world remote from the one outside.

And then there was the memory of that seemingly

demented peasant woman. Diana had been shocked by the monstrous, swarthy creature and her token of black magic. The idea of having her lurking about the shadowed old house wasn't pleasing.

She said, "I'm not sure this opportunity is right for me."

"You are an editor."

"Yes."

"The work shouldn't be demanding," the doctor argued.

"It's not that," she said with some embarrassment. "It's my attitude toward astrology and Madame Helene's prophecies. I'd probably never make a true believer. And that woman Anna didn't seem to like me. I'm sure living under the same roof with her wouldn't suit me."

Dr. Martin Gill smiled wisely. "I was afraid Anna upset you. Let me assure you there would be no repetition of such a sorry scene. I intend to lecture her and she listens to me."

"Perhaps so," Diana said. "I'm still dubious." She was prepared to shortly excuse herself and leave with a vague promise to consider the job. In her mind she'd already made a decision not to accept it. Even though in many ways it appealed to her.

The hawk face of the bald man continued to mirror good humor. "Please don't make up your mind before you experience the most important part of this interview. Madame Helene is expecting to see you. She's up in her apartment waiting for us at this very moment."

Conscious of the strength of his personality and slightly afraid of his powers of persuasion, she rose to make an exit as quickly as she could. "I don't think I should bother her," she protested. "There's such a small chance of my taking the position."

His sharp eyes fixed on hers in a hypnotic way. "You can't be serious about that. She'll be very hurt if you don't go up and see her for a brief time. As I've said, she's a very old lady. And she's become extremely interested in you since discovering that your birth dates correspond to the moment."

She hesitated, knowing the hesitation would be fatal to her decision to leave, then she said, "Perhaps for just a few minutes then."

"That is all I ask," Dr. Martin Gill said, taking her lightly by the arm. "I'll show you to the elevator."

They left the office for the almost complete darkness of the hallways. In a moment they had retraced their steps to the elevator. The door was open on the murkily-lighted small carriage and they stepped inside. The tall doctor closed the gate and set the elevator in motion by moving an antique-looking switch all the way backward. His hand on the switch as the elevator began its creaking, jolting passage upward at a snail's pace, he smiled for her benefit.

"Not the most modern of elevators," he said. "But it does well enough for us."

"How long have you been here?" she asked.

"About ten years," Dr. Martin Gill said. "Before that we had our headquarters in San Francisco. But I have found the East Coast more centrally located for our mailings to all parts of the world."

"Is the Madame a native Californinan?" Diana wanted to know.

The doctor shook his head. "No. She was born in India. She is a member of a titled British family though she refuses to trade on her family name. She's lived in America for many years."

The elevator at last reached the top floor of the old house with a jarring halt. The tall, bald doctor opened the gate for her to step out int a hall which was at least dimly lighted in contrast to the dark ones below. He was at her side again immediately to guide her down a short distance to a wide doorway leading into a very large, high-ceilinged room.

Dr. Martin Gill spoke into her ear in a subdued voice, "This was once the grand ballroom in the old days when the house was occupied by a single family. It now serves as the main room of Madame's apartment."

Diana's eyes grew wide with wonder as they entered the massive room. It was softly lighted by four great cut-glass chandeliers that drooped from the high, ornate ceiling in each quarter of the room. The walls were of some rich, brown panelled wood and along them at intervals were hung huge framed prints of Salvador Dali's twelve signs of the zodiac. Diana had used a photo of one such Dali print to illustrate her article on astrology and so at once recognized the master's work.

"Impressive," she said, studying them as they walked down the length of the hardwood floor. She'd assumed they were alone in the room but now she saw there was a darkened stage at the far end, a few steps above the floor level of the main room, and on it there was a chaise lounge on which a tiny figure reclined.

"Madame is waiting for us on the stage," the doctor said quietly.

All at once Diana had a fit of nervousness. She panicked at the thought of what she'd say to this strange person who had taken such an interest in her.

As they mounted the steps of the small stage she was able to more clearly make out the figure reclining on the couch. Madame Helene's eyes were closed as if in sleep. She was a dark-haired woman with a face strong in bone structure so that it had remained beautiful in middle-age. Diana guessed the woman must be middle-aged though it was difficult to say in the dim light of the stage. Her skin appeared white and unwrinkled and yet you knew she wasn't young. She wore an elegant gown of gold lamé, the string straps of which revealed her bare shoulders.

Diana was astonished by the woman's dress. And even more so by the way she wore her thick head of black hair. It was done up with a band of the same gold material around it and featured a glittering cluster of stones resembling diamonds and rubies in a large jewelled ornament fastened at one side. It took her a moment to think what the woman's appearance reminded her of. And then she knew. Madame Helene looked like a living effigy of one of the old time screen heroines she'd often seen in illustrations of the movies of another era. Pure camp, was her somewhat hysterical reaction to the outfit as she stood there.

Dr. Martin Gill was all solemnity and respect as he

bent over the sleeping woman and quietly said, "Madame Helene, the young woman is here."

The eyelids of the woman on the chaise lounge flicked open and the bizarrely dressed Madame Helene stared up at her without attempting to raise herself.

In a voice much more elderly than her appearance Madame Helene said, "So you are Diana Lewis!"

"Yes, I am, Madame," Diana said, drowned in embarrassment.

"You look much like your photograph," Madame Helene went on in a weary voice. "Has Martin told you what we have in mind?"

Diana nodded. "Yes."

The woman was staring at her in an odd way. "You have my birth date and I can tell you have a gift for the study of the stars. The constellations were in proper site at the time you were born."

"I appreciate the offer you've given me," Diana said. "But I don't feel I have as much talent for it as you think."

The beautiful, pale face of the oddly dressed woman on the chaise lounge showed no expression. It was strange but the ageless face of Madame Helene was almost like a rigid, frozen mask.

She said, "How can you know that without a trial? Accept the post for a month. If you aren't happy at the end of that time you can leave and no harm done."

"That wouldn't be fair to you," Diana protested.

"On the contrary," Madame Helene said calmly in that tired, almost cracked voice, "I shall be quite satisfied. I have projected myself into your future and I

37

know the great possibilities this work will open to you."

Dr. Martin Gill gave Diana a thin smile. "Madame Helene has much more confidence in you than you have in yourself."

She blushed. "So it seems."

"Today marks a high cycle for you," Madame Helene went on, "You may be hesitating to make a break and go a new way but you should have confidence in your capabilities. That is the key to the day and the weeks following."

Diana listened and at the same time let her eyes wander to take in more of the details of the stage. She saw there were two large stone urns at either end of it that were probably there for decoration. The stage was curtained in black velvet in a semi-circle. And hanging from the drapes were four gray-toned photographs blown up to giant-size of the late President John F. Kennedy, Martin Luther King, Governor Jim Denton and a singing star who had recently been killed in a head-on auto accident, Julia James.

Dr. Martin Gill must have noticed her studying the photographs. He explained, "Those are all people for whom Madame Helene predicted danger. And in the case of Governor Denton and Julia James she even made prophecies of the exact dates of their deaths."

Diana felt an eerie chill run through her. She knew from her research at the time of the article she'd written that what the hawk-faced doctor said was true. This madly dressed woman on the chaise lounge must indeed have some supernatural powers in spite of her eccentricity, for she had enhanced her reputation as a prophet by her predictions of the deaths of the governor and the singing star.

Madame Helene had closed her eyes again and in the same weary monotone, she went on, "The gifts I developed are sometimes a burden. One doesn't want to look at death. Not even another's death!"

Dr. Martin Gill touched Diana's arm. "She is very tired. We must leave her now."

Diana nodded, anxious to get away from the strange presence of the eccentric prophetess. But as they turned to leave, Madame Helene called out to her, "Please, my girl, give me one month!"

She hesitated. "I'll try," she said.

Then the doctor led her from the stage and silently along the length of the great room. Not until they were in the elevator car again on their way down, did he asked, "Well, what do you think of her?"

Diana wanted to be diplomatic. So she said, "I think she is a most unusual person."

"She is much more than that," he assured her, his shrewd eyes fixed on her. "How old do you think she is?"

"That would be hard to say," she ventured. "In her late forties or perhaps fifties. Though she looks young for that."

Dr. Martin Gill laughed. "I have a shock for you. Madame Helene is more than one hundred years old."

"I don't believe it!" she protested.

"I can supply you with documentary evidence," he assured her. "We don't make this public. It is one of our secrets so I'll depend on your discretion. If people knew they would be prejudiced by her age and question her judgments. The truth is she is more remarkable in her mental powers than ever before. Though I must admit age has sapped her of her strength."

Diana was frowning. "I felt there was something strange about her and in her way of dressing."

The face of the man beside her in the elevator showed amusement. "She has lost all contact with the changing styles. She insists on having dresses of the design of fifty years back and she has a hair-do in the same fashion."

Diana shook her head. "It's too fantastic."

"Think of the opportunity you're being offered," he said. "A chance to work for one of the truly unusual personalities of this time. I don't see how you can afford to brush it aside. That woman upstairs believes in you and your potentialities."

She stared at him. And of course she couldn't help wondering if it mightn't be all part of a giant hoax, that Madame Helene pretended to be of a great age to impress her followers. But the fact she kept it a secret spoiled that theory. She clung to anonymity to such an extent that she never even allowed her photograph to appear on her charts. Just that silhouette.

She said, "This has happened so quickly. It's hard to make up my mind."

Doctor Martin Gill said, "She only asks for a month. You can leave after that if you like." The elevator came to a halt. "I'll show you your second floor apartment."

Diana stepped out into another of the dark corridors and this time he led the way. The door to the apartment was near the elevator, an advantage which he mentioned. He showed her inside and turned on the lights. The apartment was small but pleasant, consisting of a large bed-sitting room, a bathroom and a small kitchenette.

"It's very nice," she admitted.

He moved to the window and held back a drape. "You have a view of the Public Gardens," he said. "Walter Glendon was delighted with it."

"That's the young man who was the editor," she said.

"Until his death," Dr. Martin Gill agreed coming back to her.

"What happened to him?" she asked.

"I told you it was one of life's little ironies," the doctor said. "You remember the photo of Julia James you saw upstairs?"

"Yes."

"Julia was one of our most famous show business clients. She came here regularly for private readings with Madame. Walter Glendon saw a lot of her and they became close friends. So much so that they often went out together."

"I see," she said, though it still wasn't clear to her.

"On the day Julia James was killed in that head-on collision on the Mass. Pike Madame Helene warned her of imminent danger. She had already predicted it as a black day for Julia in her column. But Julia was a light-hearted girl and refused to take the warning seriously. She and Walter Glendon had planned to drive to New York. And they went ahead with their plans. He was at the wheel when they were both killed."

41

CHAPTER THREE

Diana was shocked by this revelation. Once again the chill skeletal hand of the uncanny seemed to reach out and grip her. In these very rooms a young man had lived and served the publishing empire of Madame Helene. And when the weird ageless woman had predicted that he was in danger he'd refused to listen. As Julia James had refused to listen. And so they had both gone to their deaths.

She gave a tiny shudder. "Of course it would have happened anyway," she said. "The collision I mean. Madame Helene's prediction couldn't have been all that accurate."

The tall man with the domed bald head smiled grimly. "You are welcome to think what you like. I know both young Glendon and Julia were warned."

"I read about the accident and the mention of Madame Helene's warning," she confessed. "But I put the warning business down to newspaper talk."

Dr. Martin Gill eyed her coldly. "Too many people share that kind of skepticism. Yet the pattern set for one by the stars cannot be changed. That is proven by your presence here."

She glanced around the pleasant room. "I suppose I couldn't lose much by taking the job for a month. But I won't promise to stay beyond that."

"No need to," he assured her. "Though I'd be willing to bet that you do."

"When do you want me to begin?"

"As soon as you like. The sooner the better. There's plenty of work to be done on next month's issue of the magazine."

"I'll need a little time to sort out my things and get them cleaned," she said. "Suppose we make it day after tomorrow."

"Excellent," the doctor said. "When you bring your personal things here I'll see you're given the keys to the apartment."

"I hope I'm not making a mistake," she said.

The doctor's hawk face took on a tolerant, amused look. "Of course you're not. And consider your decision inevitable. The stars decided it."

He took her down to the first floor in the creaking elevator and then escorted her along the gloomy, dark hall to the front door. As soon as he opened it she felt the rush of warm air.

She gave him a mild smile. "Out there is like another country," she said.

"Yes, that's so true," he said with a strange expression. "We'll be expecting you."

They said goodnight and she went down the worn stone steps to the sidewalk. Then she glanced back at the four-storied brick house. The oaken door had been quickly closed after her and no lights showed from the windows. The house could be deserted for all the signs of life it showed on this hot August night.

With a sigh she turned and began walking in the direction of Arlington Street and the Arlington subway station. Right up until the last minute she'd not intended to commit herself to working for Madame Helene. Then, without really understanding why, she'd said she would. And the strange Dr. Martin Gill had told her he'd known she was going to take the job from the beginning. Madame Helene had made one of her predictions to that effect.

The street was fairly well filled with people. From the Public Gardens there came the sound of summer night talk and easy laughter. Traffic moved relentlessly along the wide street. She paused at the windows of several smart women's shops that were on the way and studied the latest styles. Her own reflection in one of the windows struck her as rather forlorn. But she pushed the thought to the back of her mind and hurried to the subway.

Steep steps leading down to a bedlam of careening trains, the sudden scream of brakes, the clang of doors automatically hurled open. The rush of footsteps mingled with subdued conversation. The smell of dampness and stale odor of humans mingled with an enveloping stench of oil. That was the world of the Boston subway in which she so often found herself. She waited for the proper train and then stepped up into it and located a seat. The train was only partly filled on this hot night when most sensible people were at home by their air-conditioners struggling to keep cool.

The scattered people in the car were hot, weary and

miserable. They sat staring blankly into space with bored faces. When the car halted at the Symphony and the stops beyond some of them briefly came to life and showed enough animation to get quickly out of the car. They were then replaced by others who seated themselves and at once lapsed into the apathetic trance induced by the swaying, noisy train.

As Diana sat there her mind was not lulled into a blank. Though she leaned this way or that slightly with the motion of the train her brain was very alert. She was thinking of that dark old house, the strangely dominating doctor and the weird old woman in an expensive dress of another age stretched out on the chaise lounge. The whole business had been like a mad dream!

Yet she'd agreed to become part of it for a month at least. The business of the prophecies fascinated her. Being in the house would give her an opportunity to study the eccentric but weirdly-gifted Madame Helene and learn something of the astrological forecast business. According to Dr. Martin Gill their interest in her had started with the publication of her article and her picture and history included with it. Following that, Madame Helene had used her supernatural powers to analyze her from a distance and guide her to the house on Beacon Street.

She knew there was a lot more to it than she understood at the moment. But she also felt these eccentrics were harmless enough. Most faddists were. The supernatural, however, was being introduced in a frightening way in the predictions of Madame Helene, especially when deaths were prophesied as in the cases of

45

that young editor and the singer, Julia James. What was it Madame Helene had murmured? That foresight of the death of others was a frightening burden.

No doubt this could be true if the old woman was haunted by such visions. But Diana was not convinced this was the case. Either Madame Helene was a mad old woman in an elegant 1920's gown or she was an actual medium of sorts, gifted with supernatural ability or ESP or whatever you wanted to term it and able to tune in on wavelengths other than those known by ordinary people.

Dr. Martin Gill's claim that the ageless beauty of Madame Helene's pale white face was of a century-old vintage also struck Diana as dubious. The tall, hawk-faced doctor had the easy, glib ways of a charlatan though he could be sincere. But he was also twisted, living with memories of his past glory in Hollywood as doctor to those luminaries of another era. The parade of autographed photos, like smiling ghosts, on his office wall underlined that.

Perhaps it was the heat and nothing else that had made her decide to throw her lot in with these strange people she decided wryly. The old house had been delightfully cool and there was air-conditioning in the apartment allotted to her. The miserable hot hours she faced at home in Brookline during the night would be an ordeal. But tomorrow she'd begin getting her things ready for the move to Beacon Street the following morning.

She knew Adam would not approve and there would be an argument between them; she was in a mood not to care. She had made up her mind and she was not going to change it. She also knew she could only tell him a part of what she'd heard and seen in the house on Beacon Street. Otherwise he'd make such a fuss she'd really have a situation on her hands.

The train halted at her stop and she got off. That night her uneasy sleep was filled with wild dreams in which Dr. Martin Gill, the monstrous, swarthy Anna and the bizarre figure of Madame Helene in gold lamé gown and hairband with jewels played strange roles. They alternately threatened her and cajoled her in the dark corridors of the enormous old mansion. One terrifying sequence followed another until she awoke limp and exhausted to another humid morning.

She filled the day in packing and preparing to close the apartment. A call to the renting agent left word for the absent owner. She also phoned Adam and he suggested they meet downtown and go to a favorite French restaurant, Du Barry's on Newbury Street. It had air-conditioning and if there were any breeze, a garden section in the rear was pleasant for open-air eating.

Adam was waiting for her when she arrived at the restaurant shortly after six. He was wearing a thin fawn summer suit and looked reasonably cool. He greeted her with, "I don't think it's as warm as it was."

She smiled wryly. "I haven't noticed any change." She had the white dress with black trim at the arms and neck. White seemed to have the psychological effect of making her seem cooler.

After some debate they decided to eat in the air-conditioned section of the basement restaurant. The wine was good and the food excellent. She waited until

47

they had enjoyed their entree of filet of sole before breaking the news that she was taking the job, reasoning that in this way the entire dinner wouldn't be ruined.

Adam scowled and said, "I was afraid you'd do that."

"It's a wonderful chance to study Madame Helene," she pointed out. "I might be able to do an important article on her for *Look* or some of the other big-paying publications. Or even a book. Who knows?"

"I don't like the kind of racket they are operating," the blond young man said. "It's disgusting the way they latched onto the Kennedy assassination and then the killing of Martin Luther King. Doing it after the fact, I may add."

"But she did predict the deaths of Governor Denton and singer Julia James to the very day."

"Pure coincidence!"

"I don't know," she sighed. "They were both clients of hers and she'd made a study of them. I think there's more to it than you want to admit. And that's why I'm taking the job. To find out."

"You may find out more than you guess," was his dark warning.

She smiled at him across the table. "I wish you wouldn't be so grim about it. You'd think it was a matter of life or death. I'm only taking the post on a month's trial basis."

Adam still looked unhappy. "I'm thinking of that living-in business. I don't like that."

"It's actually the same as if I'd rented an apartment in the area," she said. "I have my own rooms with a lock to the main door and, wonder of wonders, it has central air-conditioning built in."

He sat back and eyes her. "I honestly think you'd take on any kind of job that offered you air-conditioned surroundings. This heat spell isn't going to last."

"There are quite a few weeks ahead when it can be bad."

"The point I wanted to make about the apartment," he said, "is that it is in the same building where you'll be working. The same building where the others are living. You have to enter and leave the building by one front door. So they can keep tabs on you all the time."

"Why should they want to?"

"I don't know," he admitted. "But I think what they're doing borders on the dishonest and I hate to see you involved."

"Just try to forget all about it," she said. "If I have any problems I can always get in touch with you."

His handsome face registered concern. "That's another thing that has me bothered. I'm going to be away for at least a few weeks. I'm being sent to the New York office tomorrow. I don't know for how long."

This news was unexpected and somewhat worrying. She did count on Adam, especially at a time like this. And now he wasn't going to be around. But she was determined to hide her feelings of uneasiness saying, "That's nothing to be upset about. I can always phone you long distance and you can be here in a couple of hours using a shuttle flight."

Adam stared at her glumly. "Providing they let you phone me!" he said with grim meaning.

49

She shook her head in resignation. "Now you're being ridiculously melodramatic."

The main argument between them ending in a state of unhappy stalemate, the rest of the evening went better. They strolled along Newbury Street after darkness came. And Adam had been right—the weather was cooler as if even nature was making an effort to sway her in her decision. They went into the exclusive Ritz Hotel and she bought a needed lipstick in the drug store. By that time they were ready to stroll back to the Exeter Theatre where an Ingmar Bergman movie was playing. They were both Bergman buffs.

Because she made some complaining mention of the subway during the evening Adam insisted on taking her home by taxi. She protested and felt guilty about costing him the extra expense but he wouldn't be swayed. Their goodnight was a little longer and more tender than usual. And when Adam left he promised to keep in touch with her by letters and the phone. Diana watched the blond young man go with a hollow feeling. She would have been indignant if anyone had accused her of being afraid of entering on her new venture without him nearby for support. But it was perilously close to the truth.

Next morning the taxi she'd ordered deposited her before the house on Beacon Street and she had the driver bring out her four bags and take them up to the door. When she rang the bell it was answered by the colorless, gray-haired woman who had met her the first night.

The woman frowned at the cabby and the bags. She

said, "He can leave them in the hall inside. We'll look after them from there."

"He's willing to take them up to my apartment," she said. "That way no one here will be bothered. I've paid him for it."

The prim, gray-haired woman was adamant. "We do not allow tradespeople beyond the entrance. It is a policy laid down by Dr. Gill."

Diana raised her eyebrows. "Very well," she said. "I was only trying to help." And she had the taxi driver leave the four bags just on the other side of the door.

When he left the prim Miss Carlton said, "Dr. Gill is in his office waiting for you. I'll see that your luggage is sent upstairs."

Diana summoned a smile. "Thank you," she said.

Miss Carlton nodded stiffly and went into her office which was just off the hallway near the front door. In that small office there was the phone switchboard for the house which she attended. Diana went on down the long dark hallway to the private office of Dr. Martin Gill. The door to the office was open and the tall, hawk-faced man with the domed bald head was at his desk. Seeing her in the doorway he rose with one of his mocking smiles.

"The stars never err, Miss Lewis," he said suavely. "You are here at exactly the predicted time."

She smiled with some misgivings. "You're beginning to make me feel terribly self-conscious. I can imagine you predicting my every move."

"Don't think about it," he said. "Madame Helene and I are planning big things for you. We're anxious to help you." He held up a weighty book he'd had opened

51

on the desk before him. "Do you know anything about hypnotism?"

"Not really," she said. "I was going to do an article on its use in medicine one time but I didn't get around to it."

"Too bad," the doctor said. "It's being used more by doctors and hospitals every day. I fancy myself as something of a hypnotist and often used it when I was in regular practice rather than routine anesthesia. You'd be amazed at the excellent results I had. It's a boon when the patient has a history of heart trouble. No need to strain the organ under the load of a heavy anesthesia."

"I can imagine," she said, regarding the tall man with interest. "If you enjoyed your practice so much why did you give it up?"

His smile was thoughtful. "I sometimes ask myself the same question, Miss Lewis. And since we dispense with formality here may I take the liberty of addressing you as Diana?"

"Why not?"

"Thank you," he said. "The truth is, Diana, that I was overwhelmed by the personality of Madame Helene. From the moment I met her I knew she had extra powers of ESP plus a fine tuning to the beyond. Combine those with her abilities in making routine astrological forecasts and you have a remarkable combination."

"Indeed," she agreed.

"I have admitted you to the inner circle secret of Madame's age," he went on glibly. "So I will also give you the further confidential information that in recent years her heart has weakened greatly. She has had a series of mild attacks and the only safe way to look after her is to have a trained physician available constantly. In addition to being the Madame's associate I am also her doctor."

Diana considered this. "So you are actually dedicating your life and career to her."

"I can think of no more worthwhile purpose," the tall, hawk-faced man said. Again he was dressed neatly in a dark suit with a pin stripe and a gray striped shirt and matching tie.

"My bags are in the hall," she said. "Miss Carlton said she'd send them to my room."

"No doubt Anna has taken them up by this time."

"Anna?" she said the Italian woman's name uneasily.

Dr. Martin Gill raised a perfectly manicured hand in a gesture for patience. "You mustn't hold the other evening against her. I've talked to her and she understands you're to be one of the household."

Diana still wasn't much reassured. She asked, "What about the key to my apartment? Does she have it?"

"She will leave it on the dresser," the suave doctor told her. "I know you want to settle in so you may take as much of the morning as you need to unpack."

"I won't be too long," she promised. "I'll be glad to come down and get a start on the magazine work before lunch."

"About your meals," Dr. Martin Gill said. "You'll be taking them in the dining room with me. Miss Carlton has breakfast and dinner at home and Madame takes all her meals alone in her apartment. We don't have a regular luncheon here but I do have a break for coffee, bread and cheese. If you prefer to have anything else, you can tell Anna. She looks after the cooking and the operating of the household."

"I see," she said. And she tried to conceal the fact that this added information about the important role the monstrous Anna played in the strange household wasn't giving her much cheer. She disliked and distrusted the sullen woman whom the doctor had admitted was at least mentally slow. "You place a great deal of reliance on this Anna."

He nodded. "Like all people of limited intelligence she does very well as long as she's given minute and detailed instructions. Her ability to reason or work on her own is nil. But we give her close supervision and she has been a wonderful worker."

Diana saw that it was useless to hope she'd be able to avoid the weird peasant woman. Dr. Gill plainly had no intentions of replacing her. So she said, "I won't waste any more time. I'll go up to the apartment. I'll not have any trouble operating the elevator on my own, will I?"

"No," he said. "The sooner you become accustomed to it the better. It's clearly indicated which controls to use. I'll see you again when you come down."

She left the office in an uneasy frame of mind. As she walked down the dark corridor to the elevator, she began to have second thoughts about her decision to take on the duties of editor for Madame Helene. The doctor had been frank and pleasant enough yet she sensed an iron hand concealed behind his amiable facade. Already he was laying down the rules and there would undoubtedly be a good deal more of this. She had no idea how important a role the aged Madame Helene played in the affairs of the astrological empire but she would be willing to bet that the final authority rested in the well-manicured hands of Dr. Martin Gill.

The elevator was waiting and empty. She got into the cage and carefully followed instructions in closing the door and operating the switch. It responded to her efforts by groaning its way up to the second floor. She got off and walked the few steps to the door of her apartment and saw that it was partly ajar. With a slight frown she opened the door all the way and went inside.

What she saw made her go tense with anger. Her bags had been deposited in the room. And one of them, which she'd not been able to lock, was opened on the bed with the stout Anna bent over it pawing through the contents.

"What are you doing?" she asked the big, swarthy woman sharply.

Anna raised her head with its unkempt wiry hair and a malevolent smile crossed her broad, swarthy face. "Putting clothes away," she said in accented English and pointed to an open dresser drawer.

Diana was over beside the big woman now. "I don't need you to do that," she stressed. "I don't want you to do it. All I need is the key and you can go!"

Anna still kept her taunting smile as she stood there doing nothing for a moment. Then one of her powerful hands rummaged in a pocket in the dark sack-like dress she was wearing and she brought out the apartment key and handed it to Diana.

"You may go," Diana said, still regrding the peasant woman sternly.

Anna lost her smile and sullenly ambled out of the apartment leaving the door open after her. Diana crossed to the door and pushed it closed. The episode had been thoroughly unpleasant. She could see that one of the problems she'd face in the ancient house would be Anna. Going back to the open bag on the bed she began to sort out the things the swarthy woman had gone over and mussed. A quick examination proved that she had only used the open drawer as an excuse for going through the bag. Nothing had been transferred to the dresser.

The business of unpacking took more time than Diana had expected. And all the while she worked she kept thinking of what Anna had done and feeling angry about it. What really troubled her was whether the swarthy woman had carried out this spying on her own or at the instigation of the doctor or someone else in the house. When you were dealing with a mentality such as Anna's it was hard to tell.

In any case it made her uneasy. And another disturbing thought came to her. Since Anna was seemingly the only domestic in the mansion it was likely she was expected to clean the apartment at intervals. Diana resented such possible intrusions on her privacy and made up her mind to tell Dr. Martin Gill so. While she remained in the apartment she would take care of her own housekeeping and cleaning. She didn't care whether this attitude on her part was resented or not.

She was in the final stages of putting her things

away when she opened the drawer of a modest writing desk in the corner of the room. She began to put some small references books and a packet of personal stationery she always carried with her into the drawer when she saw a sheet of typewriter paper with some scrawled words in lead pencil. As a matter of course she took the paper from the drawer and studied its written message:

"For brief as a grain of sand falling through an hour glass is death, brief as the falling petal from a rose, so brief is the end of breath. W.G."

The intitials first caught her attention. W.G. must certainly stand for Walter Glendon, the young man who had been editor of Madame Helene's magazine before her, and who had been killed in the car accident with Julia James. She frowned, staring at the scrawled message again, as she realized this must have been written shortly before his fatal accident.

Why should he have been so obsessed with death? It would certainly indicate that he must have had a morbid streak or was it that he had some eerie premonition of his approaching death? In this strange house it was hard to guess. Dr. Martin Gill had made some reference to Madame Helene's warning the young man of grave personal danger or death for Julia James on the day he'd chosen to drive her to New York. Had that been enough to make him put down these morbid conjecturings? Perhaps.

It was, in a way, like a message from the dead. And it suddenly gave her a feeling that the tiny apartment was still tenanted by the spirit of her young male predecessor. She'd not given him much thought before

57

other than to feel sorrow that he had met such a sudden and violent end. Now she was thinking of him as a living person and wondering what sort of man he had been.

Surely his coming to work for Madame Helene had directly led to his death. Had he not been in the grim old mansion he wouldn't have met the singing star, Julia James. And it was through her he'd been killed. Diana had no sooner arrived at this conclusion than a chilling surge went through her. In thinking that she'd automatically accepted that Madame Helene's prediction of a dire fate for Julia James had been correct, she was converting to belief in the ancient seer.

Walter Glendon couldn't have shared that belief or he wouldn't have defied the prophecy to go off with Julia James on that fateful day. Or had he believed too well and knowingly placed himself in danger? The note he'd left could very easily suggest fatalism on his part.

She carefully folded the sheet of paper and placed it in the pocket of her dress. Then she finished with her unpacking. But the note went on haunting her in an odd way. So much so that she decided to show it to Dr. Martin Gill, feeling sure he would be at least able to give her some explanation of what Walter Glendon had been like. And what could have prompted him to write those few lines.

This time she found the stairway and walked down rather than use the elevator. The stairway was broad and near the front of the old house. It brought her out on the ground floor near the doorway to the prim Miss Carlton's office. And she saw that the sedate gray-haired woman was busy at the switchboard. Apparently a good number of phone calls came into this quiet headquarters of Madame Helene.

Diana went along the shadowed hallway to the office of Dr. Martin Gill. It was becoming a familiar journey now. She found the door still open and the doctor busy at one of the filing cabinets, apparently searching for some record card. He glanced her way when she entered.

"You're back sooner than I expected," he said. "All settled in?"

"Yes," she said. "It didn't take long. About Anna—," she paused in mid-sentence.

The suave hawk-faced man turned to her, a file card in his hand. His shrew eyes fixed on her. "What about Anna?"

"I'm afraid we're not going to get along."

"You mustn't worry about it," he said, standing there. "I told you I would see she behaved."

"It's just that I'd rather she wouldn't have access to my apartment at all," she said. "She makes me uneasy and I can take care of the cleaning on my own."

He shrugged. "If you like. I'll tell her."

"I wish you would," she said. "And there is something else. I found a written message from Walter Glendon in the drawer of the writing desk. A rather odd message."

The man with the domed bald head looked disconcerted. "A message from Walter? What sort of message?"

"I have it here," she said, taking it from her pocket.

He came to her quickly with a scowl on his hawk face and practically snatched the sheet of typewriter paper from her hands as he said, "Let me read it!"

CHAPTER FOUR

The doctor's rude behaviour stunned Diana. In a matter of seconds he had changed from the suave professional to an enraged boor. She stood there white and silent as he quickly scanned the sheet with its few written words. Then she saw him relax and become his assured self again as he saw what was on the paper. It was a remarkable and illuminating exhibition.

He looked up from the paper to her and said, "Why, this is nothing!"

"I don't think I suggested that it was earth shaking," she said in a quiet voice. She was disgusted with his actions and wanted to give him some hint of her feelings.

The hawk face showed a forced smile. "I'm sorry I became so excited," Dr. Martin Gill said, folding the sheet of typewriter paper and stuffing it casually in a side pocket of his suit. "I thought Walter might have left some important message for us though I should have known that wasn't the case."

She raised her eyebrows. "I'm not sure that I understand."

Dr. Martin Gill spread out his hands, "You've read those phrases of his. What do they suggest to you?"

"I can't honestly say," she was willing to admit. "Perhaps a morbidity, an excessive preoccupation with death."

"You're more than partly right," he agreed with an air of cynicism. "I didn't realize it when we hired him for the magazine but Walter was neurotic. A very uptight young man even then on the brink of a nervous breakdown. He did his work well here but I always worried about him. He fancied himself as a poet and I expect what you found was one of his abortive attempts to express himself in poetic form."

"I didn't know anything about him," she said. "I began to wonder if the phrases had anything to do with his guessing he was close to death. Whether Madame Helene had predicted his death, in fact."

The bald man's lip curled in derision. "Madame Helene had no time for him. She is much too busy developing the horoscopes of the top stars of the entertainment world and the millionaire businessmen who depend on her."

"It was just an idea," she said, resenting his overbearing explanation.

He seemed to sense this and at once was all pleasant tact again. "I can understand that you would think something of the kind. This young man is living in a house devoted to prophecy and he ponders on his approaching death. Of course you'd decide that Madame had given him some sort of warning. But she hadn't."

She studied the hawk face of the tall man. "It was

61

Julia James she had said would die on that certain day."

"Indeed it was. Julia was a regular client. I took Walter aside when he spoke of driving to New York with the girl and reminded him of the Madame's prediction. He just made light of it. So I didn't try to dissuade him."

"So he wasn't an apostle of astrology?"

Dr. Martin Gill spread his hands. "I thought he was. But it seemed not. Of course he had a great crush on Julia. It meant a great deal to him that a girl of her popularity and fame should pay any attention to him. I believe she persuaded him to go with her and he'd do anything she'd suggest."

Diana frowned. "But wasn't he the one driving when the crash occurred?"

"I believe so, though I'm not positive," was the casual reply of the man in the immaculate gray suit. "It was a tragic thing. Both Madame and I were shocked."

"The truth of her prediction must have made her much more respected by the newspaper readers of her column," Diana said. "And all her other clients."

He nodded gloomily. "We did receive a tremendous response," he admitted. "It was the same as when Madame warned of the day on which Governor Denton would be in deadly danger. When he was assassinated the press went wild."

She smiled with grim understanding. "They would be bound to. It smacks of black magic."

Dr. Martin Gill shook his head. "No. It's much more scientific than that. You see Madame Helene as merely an ailing old woman who has lived beyond her allotted span. A woman who has developed a great ability to produce accurate astrological guides. But she is much more than that. She has a genius for ESP and a communion with the world of spirits. Madame Helene is the sort of unique human who appears on the earth every two or three centuries."

Diana heard him out with a kind of bitter fascination. He was addressing her in the manner he might have used in conducting a huge meeting. His glibness had caught him up in the spell of his own oratory. The shrewd eyes glittered wildly.

She couldn't resist the opportunity of deflating him. And so she said, "But Madame Helene is human. She will certainly die one day soon. What then?"

He stood there in stunned reaction to her words. His hawk face took on a strange look. The powerful manicured hands that hung limply at his sides clenched and unclenched. She thought he'd stand there staring at her forever.

But then he found his voice. In a low tone, he replied, "Her work cannot die with her. The harvest of her genius will not be lost. We will find someone under her favored sign, someone whose talents can be developed and our mission will go on. The day will come when astrology will play a major role in the order and working of a better world. Madame Helene's philosophy will surely play a part of such a crusade."

She saw that she'd upset him and felt that perhaps she'd gone too far. So she was quick to tell him, "I shouldn't have brought the subject up."

Dr. Martin Gill had regained all his poise. He eyed

her oddly and said, "Not at all. I think it is interesting that you should. You are a perceptive young woman. And now if you'll follow me I'll take you to your office."

The room he showed her to adjoined his office but was a lot smaller. It shared the same drab gray paint job but there were none of that rank of deceased film stars to liven the walls with their ghostly smiles. There was a desk piled high with unfiled letters, reference books and copies of the magazine. A large table in the corner also stacked heavily with back issues of the magazine, several steel filing cabinets similar to the ones in the doctor's room, a swivel chair behind the steel desk and two plain chairs. There was no rug on the hardwood floor and the single high, narrow window had no drapes but panes of mottled glass which cut off any view but provided good light.

Dr. Martin Gill went over to the desk and said, "You'll find everything in a mess. I've been trying to carry on this operation with one hand since we lost Walter."

"I understand," she said.

He picked up a copy of the magazine which had a yellow cover, the title, "MADAME HELENE'S ASTROLOGICAL GUIDE, in large red lettering, along with illustrations of the signs of the zodiac and their names set out in neat columns of six at either side of the cover in blue ink. The names of contributors and the titles of their articles were featured in red type between the two columns. Diana had noticed the magazine on the newsstands but she'd never paid much attention to it.

Passing the magazine to her, he said, "That's the July issue. The September one is already with the publishers. I've got the November one started but you'll be expected to complete it and take over the January issue on your own."

She gave him a wise smile. "You forget I'm only here a month on trial."

"Not really," he said. "I hope you're going to like the work well enough to stay. Your name will go on the November masthead as editor."

After a few minutes he left her to study copies of the magazine. He promised to give her some time in the afternoon, showing her what he'd done for the November issue so she could complete assembling the material for it. He explained that most of the articles were written either by him or Madame Helene, using various pen names. The items reprinted from other newspapers and magazines of a news nature would be her responsibility. But the editorials and main articles would all be provided by him.

She settled down at the desk with a sigh. The general mayhem of its top made her loath to attempt straightening out the tangled mess of letters and copy material. She decided she'd begin by making herself familiar with the magazine. It wasn't large—numbering an average of twenty-eight pages. There was no outside advertising, only offerings from the Madame Helene organization. But these were numerous and she judged probably drew handsome returns in cash.

One advertisement dealt with an involved monthly horoscope service paid for in monthly installments that would total more than a hundred dollars over the year.

Another offered Madame Helene's Hints For Astro Beauty, while an even more sensational one was devoted to a service guaranteed to solve sex problems of individuals or couples with the aid of the stars. All designed to bring in a steady flow of cash.

Diana found the familiar black silhouette of Madame Helene over the masthead of the magazine on page three. The astrologist was listed as Editor. Beneath her name was that of Dr. Martin Gill as Managing Editor. This was the post the last Walter Glendon had held and which she was taking over. She skimmed through the pages getting an idea of the type of articles used. The only column she bothered to read in detail was one simply called: Predictions. In it Madame Helene indulged in various prophecies, none of them definite enough to get her in trouble with the exception of one. The Madame went on record as definitely predicting there would be a hippie riot in the Public Gardens on the Last Sunday in August. Diana's eyebrows raised as she realized this wasn't too far away. And of course she wondered if the riot really would take place.

After finishing the current issue of the bi-monthly she began to go back through earlier issues. And it was through this that she came upon the rather fuzzy photo of Walter Glendon under the masthead of the editorial column. The photo was small and showed a rather weak-faced young man with bushy blond hair, a receding chin and sad eyes. For some reason the photo was dropped from subsequent issues even before the editor's tragic death was noted in a box with a black border.

Because of her earlier discovery of the few lines left by the young editor she was especially interested in the photo. She studied it for quite a long while until an impression of his face was registered on her mind. As she put the copy of the magazine aside she saw that it was close to one o'clock. She decided she would like some milk and perhaps a light sandwich of some sort. The thought that she would have to go to the kitchen and brave Anna to get it didn't cheer her up.

There had been no sound from the office next door for quite some time so she guessed that Dr. Martin Gill had gone to some distant part of the house or perhaps out somewhere. She left her desk and went out into the hall to find the kitchen. The halls were almost as shadowed and gloomy in daylight as they were at night. And the deathly silence she'd noticed when she first entered the ancient house still bothered her.

Going by the open door of Dr. Martin Gill's office she saw that it was empty. She was on her way past the elevator when the gate was thrown back and the weirdly dressed figure of Madame Helene emerged from the cage. The beautiful but oddly pale and unwrinkled face of the old woman held its usual rigid, staring expression. Her eyes fixed on Diana as if she did not remember her. There was an uncertainty in her manner. She was wearing a long gray dress with elegant ostrich feather trim on the mid-length sleeves. Her hair was gathered up in the bizarre style of the 1920s to match her gown.

Madame Helene spoke in a hushed tone, asking, "Where is Martin?"

"I think Dr. Gill is out somewhere," Diana said. "I imagine Miss Carlton would know."

Fear clouded the eyes of the ridiculously garbed old woman. A tiny hand with the mottled skin of the very old pressed against her heart in a dramatic gesture. "He shouldn't leave me!"

"Is there anything I can do?" Diana asked politely. The astrologist seemed to be trembling and, remembering her heart condition, Diana began to worry she might be about to have an attack.

Madame Helene kept staring at her as she swayed ever so slightly. "Who are you?" she asked in that near whisper.

Diana managed a smile. "I'm Miss Lewis. You must remember. You hired me to edit the magazine the other day."

The old woman with the harshly dyed black hair looked at her oddly. "We met at the Fairbanks party," she ventured in a nervous manner.

"I'm afraid not."

"You were with D. W. Griffith," Madame Helene went on. "Of course I say he is the best director of them all." She looked up and down the corridor unhappily. "I must find Martin! Where is he?" Near panic seemed to have seized the old woman.

Diana was about to offer her help once again when the huge form of Anna came waddling down the hallway out of the shadows. The old woman gave a gasp of pleasure at seeing the giant Italian woman. Anna glared at Diana and with murmurings of displeasure bundled Madame Helene back into the elevator and slammed the gate closed in Diana's face. Almost at once the elevator began creaking its way upstairs.

She stood there hardly believing what had just taken place. The other evening Madame Helene had struck her as eccentric and out-of-touch with styles. But just now she'd behaved like someone with a fogged mind. The references to Douglas Fairbanks and D. W. Griffith proved her ancient brain was wandering back to the early days of Hollywood, the silent film period. No doubt she had lived in the film capital and met Dr. Martin Gill, physician to the stars.

It was a discovery of some enormity to learn that the old woman's mind was no longer stable. While there was a possibility Madame Helene might have periods when her mind was clear and capable, the evidence was all that the hawk-faced Gill manipulated her and the empire. The ancient astrologer was probably only a puppet for the doctor to use as a front. The predictions and all the real work were likely his.

She found her way to the kitchen troubled by these thoughts. From all she'd seen and heard she began to agree with Adam Purcell. That young man had been right when he'd accused Dr. Gill and the Madame of being charlatans. There could hardly be any other way to describe what they were doing. No doubt many honest astrologers existed—men and women who worked along strictly scientific lines to produce their findings. But this was not the case with the Madame Helene organization.

It had become big business. She'd never seen the publishing plant or the main office on Washington

Street but she was sure there would be a great many employed there and the turnover of material must be tremendous. The predictions with which Madame Helene had been so lucky and the emphasis on ESP and spiritualism moved her from the astrological ranks into a limbo where exploitation of the gullible was the rule.

In the kitchen she went to the refrigerator and discovered a supply of milk. There was bread in a box and plenty of canned goods. She settled for pouring herself a glass of milk and making herself a sardine sandwich. Taking them back to her office she ate in silence and peace as she leafed through other magazines.

After lunch she began to clean up her desk; it was no mean task. In fact she was still occupied with it around three o'clock when Dr. Martin Gill presented himself in her office.

She smiled up at him and pushed back a straying lock of hair as she paused in attempting to place some of the letters in proper order. "This is worse than I expected," she said.

He came over to the desk and glanced at what she was doing. "You're at the hardest part of it now," he said by way of encouragement. "By tomorrow you'll be getting on with your own work."

"I hope so," she said. "By the way, around lunch hour Madame Helene was down here looking for you."

The hawk face shadowed. "I know. I've just come from up there. These days I hardly dare leave the house. It's becoming very difficult."

70

"She seemed unwell," Diana said tactfully, wondering if the reticent doctor would offer any further comment.

"She shouldn't wander about the house. It's dangerous for her. I've warned her about using the elevator."

"I offered to help her," Diana said, throwing out more bait. "But I don't believe she remembered me."

Dr. Martin Gill gave her a stern look. "You can hardly criticize someone over a hundred years old for forgetting details occasionally."

Diana was on her feet now. "I had no intention of criticizing."

"Of course you didn't," the suave doctor said in his glib way. "It is true that every so often Madame Helene's mind wanders. She begins living in the past. The spells don't last long. Then she is as alert as ever. Though I must admit she is terrified by the lapses and very embarrassed about them. So you mustn't ever mention them."

"I won't."

His eyes took on that fanatical glitter. "She can still lead and sway an audience when she's rested and well. You may find that hard to believe but it is true."

She was interested enough to ask, "Does Madame make many public appearances?"

"She never leaves this building anymore," Dr. Martin Gill said. "But we hold group meetings in that big room up in her apartment. We often have as many as twenty or thirty people in attendance. Whenever she feels up to it Madame Helene gives the lecture person-

71

ally. And the response she gets is always more enthusiastic than when I take her place."

"I can well believe that," Diana said.

His eyes fixed on her. "You Geminis are all much alike. You have a deep sincerity and the ability to communicate well. I can see those qualities in you as I see them in the Madame."

She was a trifle embarrassed at this unexpected comparison. But she supposed it wasn't too unusual coming from someone who built his whole career on a foundation of the art and science of the stars.

Changing the subject she began to question him about the November issue of the magazine and they were soon in a serious discussion of its makeup. He spent more than an hour bringing her up-to-date on the material and left her with a much better understanding of her job.

At the door he halted to say, "Always lock up anything of value before you leave your office. I make a point of placing my papers in the wall safe whenever I'm absent from my desk."

"I'll remember," she said. "And thank you."

"A pleasure," he smiled. His hawk face could take on a magnetic attraction when he wished it to. "You will notice some callers all through the day and every day of the week. These are my private clients whom I treat hypnotically as well as guiding them by means of the stars."

"You have great faith in hypnosis," she ventured.

"I have seen it accomplish miraculous things in mental and physical healing," he went on in his convincing way.

"I would like to watch you giving a treatment one day," she said.

Those shrewd, overpowering eyes met hers directly. "Better still," he suggested, "allow me to demonstrate on you. It's the most satisfactory way."

"Thank you," she said politely, though she had reservations about being hypnotized. And she'd be especially against it while living in these strange surroundings.

After the doctor left her she continued with her work until it was late in the afternoon. Miss Carlton came with the letters that had arrived in the mail. The prim woman with the iron-gray hair was in a disgruntled mood. "Wanted me to work tonight," she said indignantly as she took letters from a wire basket she carried and placed them on Diana's desk. "He is having one of those meetings! I said I wouldn't stay around here until midnight and long after to please anyone."

"Meetings?"

"The group lectures," the prim woman sniffed. "I can tell you it's a mixed lot that shows up. I say it's all right to deal with that sort through the mail but I don't cotton to having them brought here intruding on us."

"Dr. Gill mentioned the meetings."

"You'll find out!" Miss Carlton said ominously. "I say he should get some extra help. But he never listens to me. Up there with that poor old thing a lot of the time." Miss Carlton leaned closer to her and in a low confidential voice said, "She's not always right in the head, you know. And he goes up there late every afternoon and runs off old movies for her. Not the sort you see now but from the silent picture days."

Diana lifted her eyebrows. "She must be very fond of old films."

"Half the time I swear she thinks its real," the front office woman said. "I had to go up there one afternoon and I caught them at it. Watching those old movies flickering on the screen and sitting there talking and laughing about the people in them as if they were alive. And I'll bet you every single one up there on the screen must have been dead for years."

Diana smiled slightly, thinking the older woman too critical. Many people found pleasure in old movies. And she thought this hobby of Madame Helene's not nearly as important a cause for worry as the old woman's general state of mind evidenced in the way she dressed.

"All her clothes are like the ones in those silent films," Miss Carlton went on. "I say that's going too far. I wouldn't stay in this house nights for all the money they could pay me. You must be brave to want to do it."

"My apartment seems very nice."

The prim woman gave her a bleak look. "That's what Walter Glendon said." And with this enigmatic remark she went on to leave the bulk of the letters in her wire basket with Dr. Martin Gill.

Diana had absorbed all the information the prim woman had offered. Gradually she was learning more of the habits of the various people in the big mansion. She began to sort out the mail and in it found a card sent from New York by Adam. Written in his spidery

74

hand was the message, "If you don't like things now that you're in the house you needn't stay. There's no law that can make you."

She smiled bitterly to herself as she put the card carefully aside in a personal file to answer on her own time. If Adam had seen things in the mansion as starkly revealed as she had in the past few hours she was sure he'd drag her into the street without even waiting for her luggage. But she had more diplomacy than that. She was going to somehow manage until she learned all the true facts about Madame Helene. There was that expose to write either as an article or a complete book.

Five o'clock came and Miss Carlton left promptly as usual. Dr. Martin Gill came to Diana's office and advised her, "You can quit work any time you like. After five your office duties are over unless you have to do overtime to catch up."

She gave him a look of wan amusement. "I'd say I'll be in that position for some weeks."

"Don't worry about it," the hawk-faced man said. "I'm going up to spend an hour with the Madame. She looks forward to a period of conversation and entertainment at this time every day. Often I screen some favorite film for her. We have a projector installed up there."

"Madame Helene likes films?"

He nodded. "She spent some time in Hollywood at the period I did. And she has so many clients among the stars her interest in them remains strong."

"Naturally," she said. And she lifted up the current issue of the magazine to say, "I find her predictions exciting. The riot in Boston Public Gardens for instance. She says that will happen and names the date."

Dr. Martin Gill looked very calm about it. "There have been many serious riots among the young people lately both in college and out. It wouldn't surprise me if she's right about this one."

"It will be interesting to see," she said.

The doctor started for the door and then turned to say, "There is one other thing. People will be coming for our group study of the stars and their influence tonight. It would be most helpful if you'd take care of seeing them in for about a half-hour. They usually always arrive within that period."

So she was to have the job Miss Carlton had been offered as an extra and which she'd turned down. But Diana was in no position to refuse since she was a newcomer to the organization. As a matter of fact her curiosity was the one thing that made her eager to take on the responsibility. She wanted to get a closer look at Madame Helene's clients.

Dinner proved an adequate but plain meal served dourly by the big Anna. At a few minutes before eight Diana installed herself in Miss Carlton's office. She'd only been there a short time when the doorbell rang. It was the first of those attending the meeting, a short, stout man of middle-age with a bloated, merry face.

He eyed her with interest as she let him in. "You're new here," he said.

"Yes," she told him. "I assume you know your way to the elevator and how to get upstairs?"

"Sure do," the stout man chuckled. "I've been coming once a week for three or four years now.

76

The Madame is a wonderful prophet." And with that he strolled off down the hall towards the elevator.

Before he was out of sight the doorbell again rang. This time it was a well-dressed elderly couple. The man had a lean cruel face with slanted eyes and ears that came to what looked like points. The woman was nondescript. They went on and others kept arriving. They all had one thing in common besides an interest in astrology, every one of them seemed mildly eccentric. The last group to arrive were three hippie types. She was especially impressed by the leader of the trio, a brash dark-haired youth with a quick tongue.

He was wearing an anti-Viet Nam badge and offered her one which she refused. He looked at her with disdain. "Are you for the war?"

"No," she said. "I'm against it. I'm also against wearing childish badges that don't mean anything much."

That silenced him and he and his companions went on their way to the elevator. She waited for twenty minutes longer without anyone else coming. She'd counted twenty-four and felt that was all there would be. So she walked down the dark hall to the elevator to take it to the second floor and her room.

Almost as soon as she stepped into the elevator she noticed there was a strange new odor permeating the old building. It seemed to come from above and smelled a lot like a spicy rose incense. The smell seemed stronger on the second floor than it had below. And she decided it was some sort of incense the weird old Madame Helene was using for her group meeting. No doubt a bit of stage management on the crafty Dr.

Martin Gill's part to enhance the atmosphere of the gathering.

She let herself into her apartment and turned on the light. As the spicy smell also seemed prominent in there she turned on the air-conditioning to full. Then she began to prepare for bed. The day had been trying and she needed a good rest.

But this was not to be. Her sleep was tormented by dreams. Dreams that were new and strange to her. And prominent in them was the young man with the weak poet's face and sad eyes, Walter Glendon. He came close beside her bed and reached out an icy hand to grasp her in pleading fashion while his lips moved in a desperate attempt to tell her something. Pain and despair showed on that ghostly face and yet no words came from his lips. Drenched with perspiration she awoke with a scream!

CHAPTER FIVE

Diana sat up and stared into the darkness of the room with terrified eyes. The pounding of her heart sounded in her ears. Nothing else broke the silence. The ghost that had tormented her in her nightmare had vanished with her waking. But the eerie sense of the dead Walter Glendon's presence still remained there in the shadows. She had never believed in spirits but now she was forced to the conclusion the apartment must be haunted.

Her breathing was nervous and tortured. And it seemed to her that the odd spicy rose odor had penetrated into the apartment. As the initial terror of her waking subsided she gradually began to relax. And then the pressing need for sleep caused her eyelids to droop. At last she lay back on the pillow and slept again.

Two unusual things disturbed her in the morning. First, she woke with a nagging headache and she had never been subject to headaches. Secondly, she'd overslept and it was ten o'clock before she took her place in her office. When she'd passed the office of Dr. Martin Gill he'd been taking a phone call and she'd congratulated herself on not having to face him. She still had some traces of a bad head and she was thoroughly ashamed of having slept too long.

She was checking on an article for the November issue when the tall, hawk-faced man finally came in to see her. She looked up at him with a wry smile. "Your apartment is much too comfortable and quiet. I overslept this morning for the first time I can remember."

The suave Dr. Martin Gill showed no indication of concern. "Don't worry about it," he said. "Your hours are your own as long as you get your work done. And you did give us some extra time last night admitting those attending our group meeting."

"How did it go?"

"Very well, indeed," he said. "Madame spoke on Leo, the fifth sign."

She sat back in her chair. "Do you use an incense for your meetings? When I got into the elevator last night I caught the odor of something. A kind of rose perfume with a touch of spice."

He nodded with a mildly amused look. "I confess we do stage-manage things a little. You know, soft lights and background music and a touch of incense to induce a properly relaxed mood."

"I thought it was something like that."

Dr. Martin Gill furrowed his brow. "These days people expect something of a psychedelic nature, especially the younger ones. It is much less harmful to use lighting and sound effects with a harmless incense than to try and turn our clients on with some drug like LSD."

"I agree," she said. "You do have to cater to this interest in finding something new to induce experience."

"Exactly," he agreed. "Madame does not understand it. In her prime days on the West Coast the stars would come to her studio for a reading and that was that. Now these extra touches are required for a successful operation."

He went back to his own office and she returned to her magazine work. Her headache gradually vanished and she began to feel more like herself. But her energy seemed in oddly short supply, she felt an unusual lethargy. And she fought to dispel it with modest success. Memories of her nightmare kept coming back to her and once she searched for a back issue of the magazine that contained Walter Glendon's photo and stared at the unhappy, weak face in troubled fascination.

In the light of day she was sure, that it had all been a nightmare. Her feeling that the apartment was haunted could be tied in with her semi-awake state. In the dark all kinds of mad, frightening thoughts assailed you. She'd been nervous from childhood. It was stupid of her to allow a night of bad dreams to sway her in her decision to remain with this job for at least a month.

Though it was another fine, warm day the old house was so dark and cool she hadn't even thought about the heat. That was something to be thankful for. It would take her a little while to adjust to her new surroundings then she'd likely be very happy.

At lunch hour she had a meeting with the malevolent Anna. She went to the kitchen to get a glass of milk and sandwich for herself. And the big woman was lumbering about the gloomy room preparing some dish. Anna thought she should try to make some gesture of friendship towards the slow-minded peasant woman. So she stopped beside the table where she was standing over a mixing bowl.

"I don't mean to interrupt you, Anna," she said. "But I'd like to get myself a snack. I did yesterday. I know things are informal here at noon."

The beady black eyes of the big woman fastened on her. "Go to dining room," she ordered. "Anna will get."

Diana hesitated. "I don't mind helping myself."

"Anna will get," the sullen Anna insisted.

She saw that the big woman was not going to be reasonable. So very quietly, she said, "Very well. I'd like a glass of milk and toast." And she left Anna to preside over her domain.

The toast and milk finally arrived after quite a wait. Anna took them from her tray and set them on the table before Diana without a word. The peasant woman was evidently determined not to be friends with her. Diana sighed and ate her lunch alone in the shadowed dining room. Glancing around she became more aware of what she'd already realized. The old mansion was not being kept clean.

It was too much to expect of the peasant woman, Anna. And she certainly was only managing to keep things livable in a mediocre way. Dust and grime had gathered on much of the ornate woodwork and the walls. The windows were dirty and had cobwebs in their corners. The floors were not in a good state and the furniture only a little better. She had an idea Anna dusted it at long intervals. It was strange that Dr. Martin Gill did not have more help in the house. Certainly it wasn't money that held him back. Probably it was part of his desire for privacy.

In a sense the old house on Beacon Street was like a fortress. A retreat from which Madame Helene and Dr. Martin Gill ruled their empire. And it was plain enough that the shrewd doctor didn't want too many around at this headquarters. Adam had been right in terming the operation close to a racket. She was seeing it in that light more every day. And of course the wily doctor was responsible for the way things were being conducted. Madame Helene was old and faltering. Diana thought the famed astrologer should have a nurse rather than depend on Anna.

After lunch she took a few minutes to go out and visit the prim Miss Carlton in her office. The gray-haired woman glanced up from the switchboard where she sat and said, "If you're looking for Dr. Gill he's gone to the Washington Street offices. He goes over there almost every day at noon."

"I see," she said. "I really wasn't looking for him. I have plenty of work to do on my own."

Miss Carlton frowned. "That Walter Glendon was always complaining about being overworked. But then he had a lot of crazy ideas."

"Really?" She tried not to show her intense interest in this comment. Striving to sound casual she asked, "Did you find him unstable?"

"Not much better than one of those hippies," Miss Carlton said in disgust. "He came to a bad end. I knew he would." The phone rang then and their conversa-

83

tion was interrupted as Miss Carlton wrote down a message for Dr. Gill.

When Miss Carlton was free again Diana asked her, "What do you make of all this? Do you believe in astrology?"

"I don't ask any questions," was the prim woman's sharp retort.

"I didn't mean to be too personal," Diana apologized. "But I find the atmosphere here strange. And so must you since you're a very realistic person. Take Madame Helene for instance. Dr. Gill says she is over a hundred years old though she certainly doesn't look it. And her conversation is so vague and mixed up. Even he admits her mind wanders."

"A lot of the time she lives in the past," Miss Carlton was willing to admit. "But then so does he though he tries to pretend he's younger than he is. You've seen those Hollywood photos on his office walls. Every one of them signed personal and every one of the signers dead for maybe fifteen or twenty years."

"I did notice them," she agreed.

"The old woman has had her face lifted at least once since I've been here," the prim receptionist said grumpily. "Eternal beauty he calls it! But I guess we could all be eternally beautiful if we had a plastic surgeon at our elbow when we wanted him."

Diana said, "How old do you think she really is?"

"Old," was Miss Carlton's comment. "She has to be. According to her talk she was around Hollywood in the silent days."

"Dr. Gill says she was born in India of titled English parents."

84

The gray-haired woman nodded. "Maybe and maybe not. She's a mystery and that's for sure. But I don't go around asking a lot of questions. They pay well and that's all I need to know."

Diana took this as a signal for her to stop her questions. A call came in conveniently to take the older woman's attention and Diana hurried back to her office. Later, she heard Dr. Martin Gill return. It was mid-afternoon when she found herself with a problem of layout on which she felt she should consult him. She left her office and went the short distance down the hall to his.

The door was open but he wasn't at his desk. And then she noticed that the door of the walk-in safe at the far end of the room was ajar and there was a light showing from in there. She stood quietly until the tall figure of the doctor emerged from the safe door.

He looked startled for a moment. "I hope I haven't kept you waiting long. I've been checking some of our records. We keep a lot of important files in the safe. We couldn't afford to lose them in the event of fire." He carefully swung the heavy safe door closed and let it click shut. He tried the handle to make sure it was secure before crossing to join her.

She explained her problem and he gave her advice on it. She watched him carefully as he talked and saw that Miss Carlton was right. The hawk-faced, bald doctor probably was much older than she'd assumed. He could even be a well-preserved seventy. But he was extremely agile in mind and body so it was hard to tell except by association. And those signed photos of the deceased movie greats on his office walls were a give-away.

At the end of his explanation concerning the magazine, she thanked him. "I'm afraid I'm stupid in catching on to the style."

"You're doing fine," he said, his eyes studying hers with that hypnotic intensity that made her uneasy. "Last night after the meeting Madame Helene spoke to me about you. She is very pleased with you thus far."

Diana privately doubted this. She believed the old woman was far too befogged to take much interest in anything. But she pretended to accept the remark at face value. "I'm glad," she said.

"You were born under her sign," he said. "She feels close to you."

Diana excused herself as soon as possible and went back to her own desk and work. That night she wrote a letter to Adam Purcell. While she was careful not to say too much to upset him she did hint that there were things about her new job she did not like. But she told him she planned to finish out her month at least. She read it over and then put it in an envelope and stamped it.

It was after dusk and she decided to go for a short walk and mail the letter at a corner box so it would get on its way at once. Writing Adam had made her feel less uneasy and she was anxious to have an early reply. She took the elevator downstairs and left the old house.

The heat wave had come to an end. She found the walk to the corner of Arlington Street pleasant. She posted the letter and lingered on the corner for a moment to study the Public Gardens and the city in the background. The lights gave the area a touch of magic and it all seemed rather beautiful to her. And it suddenly came to her that this was the first time she'd left that strange old house on Beacon Street since she'd gone there.

With Adam out of town she had little reason to venture out in the evenings. But she realized remaining in the rather weird atmosphere of the Beacon Street mansion wasn't healthy. She must make some plans. Perhaps call Jennifer at the newspaper and see if she had an evening free. They could go out for dinner or see a movie together.

Somehow she must keep her days in balance. There was too much strain in the shadowed corridors and rooms of Madame Helene's headquarters. She had the feeling there was a lot she didn't know about the place and what went on there. And in a way she was satisfied it should be that way. There was something eerie about the old woman living in her memories and the manner in which the suave Dr. Gill pretended she was normal.

Slowly, almost reluctantly, Diana began walking back to the brick house. There was a part of her that tried to hold her back. A small voice of warning that suggested she'd be unwise to return to the house. All she had to do was take a taxi back to her apartment. She could send for her things in the morning or go get them herself. That way she'd be finished with this strange experience she'd embarked on against Adam's judgment. The shadowed street was quiet with few people on foot. She was almost ready to halt and hail a cab and run away from it all.

Then she heard the footsteps clicking on the pavement behind her. And for some reason she could not define she knew at once those footsteps had a special meaning for her. Her heart beat faster as she realized that whoever it was had to be gaining on her. She was frightened and didn't know why. Then, so suddenly it made her gasp out with fear, a hand gripped her left arm. She turned in consternation to look into the face of Dr. Martin Gill. They had come to a halt under a nearby street lamp partly covered by tree branches but enough of the mercury blue glow came through to highlight his hawk face and domed bald head. He was studying her with a smile that could be interpreted as friendly or as merely coldly triumphant.

"I hope I didn't frighten you," he said in his suave fashion.

She was temporarily annoyed. "As a matter of fact, you frightened me badly," she complained.

"I'm sorry," he said, but he still held her by the arm. "I happened to be out for a stroll myself and I saw you."

Diana didn't believe this. She had an idea he'd deliberately followed her from the house. That for some strange reason he didn't trust her. He had wanted to discover where she was going and possibly whether she was meeting anyone. Why should he be suspicious?

She said, "I wanted to mail a letter and get some air."

"We have a rather pleasant yard at the rear of the house," he said. "I'm afraid we haven't done much with it lately. Madame used to have a garden there but she lost interest in it. However, whenever you wish some air I can't think of a better place."

Frowning slightly, she said, "I also wanted to get away from the house." She resented the fact he still held her arm, though more lightly now.

His strange, hypnotic eyes fixed on hers. "I should have thought of that," he apologized. "I agree. The house can be very confining. At least we can walk back together."

She allowed him to lead her in the direction of the house. And she tried to convince herself that his explanation of their meeting being an accident had been true. Even if he had followed her there could be extenuating circumstances. An enterprise such as Madame Helene's Astrological Institute had to operate under a cloak of secrecy. And she had learned some of the inner secrets already. This meant she could, if she wished, write a kind of expose of the group. Because of that the astute doctor might think of her as a threat. But if he hadn't trusted her why had he hired her?

Dr. Martin Gill's soft voice intruded on her troubled thoughts. "I want you to attend one of the upstairs meetings soon. I'd like to have you see Madame at her best. And it would give you more insight into our methods of working."

She gave him a side glance. "Your principal motivation has to be money, doesn't it, doctor?"

He chuckled. "There's a good deal of truth in your comment. But I promise you we are a dedicated organization. One day all the world will know of us and what we are trying to do."

"If Madame survives," she pointed out.

"The organization will survive," the doctor promised. "You need not fear about that." They had reached the steps of the old house and he led her up them to the door. Fumbling in his pocket for a pass key he unlocked it. "I never depend on Anna answering," he said, allowing Diana to enter the cool, dark hall ahead of him.

She went inside feeling that she had perhaps lost her last chance for freedom. It was a ridiculous thought. She was no prisoner in the old house. But that was the way she felt and she couldn't change it.

The wily doctor had shut the door after them. "It's early yet," he said. "Surely you'll have a drink with me."

Diana hesitated, she was badly mixed up in her feelings. Curiosity prodded her to accept the drink and learn what she could about him. But her resentment at being approached by him in the street and practically dragged back made her feel she should refuse. In the end curiosity won and she accompanied him to the office lined with those smiling faces of the dead. He seated her in an easy chair and went about preparing the gin and tonic she'd asked for.

When he brought it to her she noticed the slight unsteadiness of his hand and the faint suggestion of a slur in his speaking. And it came to her as something of a shock that the tall doctor had already been drinking and likely heavily.

He had a glass of his own filled with ice and some amber liquid. Now he stood above her sipping it and smiling. "You remind me of Lily Damita," he said.

"I guess she was a famous movie star."

"Wonderful comedienne," he said, sipping his drink and then sighing. "And a grand person. We had a lot of good times together."

"Before you met Madame Helene," she said pointedly.

He showed annoyance. "Madame Helene came into my life much later. And we have never shared a romantic interest."

Diana greatly doubted this knowing how much the bizarre old woman depended on him. She had the uneasy feeling that the bald doctor was trying to impress her with his ability as a ladies' man. It was embarrassing and a little ridiculous.

"You must have enjoyed those Hollywood days," she said.

A nostalgic expression had swept across his hawk face as he turned to slowly scan the gallery of the glamorous dead. "They were my happiest days," he said.

"Was Madame Helene an astrologer then?"

He looked at her again with a wary eye. "No," he said dryly. "She was not. As I say, we met somewhat later."

"Where did you get your medical degree?" she asked.

Dr. Martin Gill sipped slowly from his glass. "Europe," he said. "I am not a native born American."

"You'd never guess it," she said. "I mean you have no accent."

His smile was bleak. "Thank you. But let us talk about you. I find you much more interesting."

She managed to appear amused and wished she could find an excuse to leave him and go up to her apartment. She said, "You've just investigated me thoroughly when you hired me. You know all my history."

The hawk face showed a new look of interest. "It is your future which chiefly concerns me," he said. "Do you know how far you can go in this organization with your talents?"

"I'm afraid you're exaggerating them," she warned him.

He came close to her to earnestly say, "I mean it."

She saw that he was drunk and not responsible. To remain there would be to court an unpleasant scene. She rose quickly and put aside her half-empty glass. "I really must go upstairs now," she said. "I'm tired."

Dr. Martin Gill made a lurching attempt to put an arm around her and she dodged neatly to one side. The hawk face registered disappointment. He said, "Diana!" And he reached for her again.

She stepped back and at the same instant the phantom-like figure of Madame Helene appeared in the doorway of the office. The old woman with the beautiful, white face like a staring mask was wearing a fancy velvet gown that reached the floor. She looked like the ghost of some long-forgotten silent movie star who had stepped out from the screen. But it was her burning eyes that caught Diana's attention.

The mad eyes were fastened on Dr. Martin Gill with an accusing gleam in them. "No!" the priestess of the astrology cult whispered hoarsely.

"What are you doing down here?" he demanded, his tone angry.

"You mustn't!" she said with a whispered intensity. Dr. Martin Gill looked unhappy and quickly went to her. "You know this is bad for you. Why did Anna allow you to come wandering down alone?"

"Scum!" Madame Helene whispered pointing the finger of one of her skinny, mottled hands at him.

"Don't call me that!" the hawk-faced Gill snarled and he gave the old woman a resounding slap across the face with his free hand.

"No!" Diana protested and went to the old woman's aid.

Madame Helene had let out a small pained moan and covered her white mask of a face with her brown mottled hands. And as Diana came close to her the old woman slumped to the floor.

"Stand back! I'll look after her," Dr. Martin Gill said. He seemed sobered by the scene and he bent down over her in professional fashion. After a second's examination he reached in an inner pocket and brought out a small glass phial. He broke it open and quickly put it under the nostrils of the woman on the floor.

It seemed an age before Madame Helene responded to the treatment to moan and stir a little. The agile doctor lifted the tiny woman in the ancient velvet dress up in his arms and told Diana, "She'll be all right now. I'll take her upstairs." And he vanished into the darkness of the hall with his burden.

Diana remained standing there watching after them.

The dramatic arrival of Madame Helene and the unexpected violence which had followed had badly upset her. And her mind was made up. She wanted no more of Dr. Martin Gill and his unsavory project. In the morning she would pack and inform him she was leaving. That determination reached she left the doctor's office and walked the length of the hall to the stairs and up to her second floor apartment.

In the apartment she bolted the door after her and went to the phone. Adam had given her his New York phone number and she felt she needed to talk to him. Needed to hear his familiar voice and let him know that she was belatedly taking his advice and leaving the sinister house on Beacon Street.

Seated by the phone she dialed the New York number directly. After a moment the phone began to ring. But no one answered it. She let it ring again and again without any results. Thinking she might have dialed the wrong number she tried once more. But still no one replied to the insistent ringing at the other end of the line. She could only assume that Adam had been sent out on a tour of accounts in other cities of New York state. The firm had often had him do that when he was headquartered in Boston. With a look of despair on her attractive face she put the phone down.

So now all she had to do was get through the night. And in her upset state it wouldn't be easy. At least she was safe in her own apartment and in the morning she'd leave as quickly as she could. She undressed and turned out the light and hoped that sleep would soon come. But it didn't. At last sheer exhaustion made her close her eyes and sleep finally followed.

But it was a broken rest. And some time later she opened her eyes to the darkness of her bedroom. She was suddenly conscious of something different in the room. Her mind flashed to a vision of the late Walter Glendon and she almost expected to see his forlorn, weak-faced ghost as she had on that other night. But it wasn't a ghost she sensed in the air this time.

It was that strange odor again. The not unpleasant combination of spice and rose petals. She breathed of it deeply and sat up in bed. Her head was reeling and she was certain the smell was much stronger than she'd ever known it to be before. The room began to spin and she lay back on her pillow and feverishly gripped the single sheet she used for covering. She was frantically clutching the sheet when she blacked out.

When she opened her eyes again there was daylight in the room. The weird odor of spice and roses had vanished but she felt dizzy and ill. She was actually too weak to lift herself up in bed. She panicked at this realization. Struggles to raise herself came to nothing. She fell back exhausted with perspiration streaming down her temples. She couldn't understand it.

What amazed her even more was to see the door of her apartment open and Dr. Martin Gill come striding in with a purposeful look on his lean, hawk's face. He came directly across to her bed and took her pulse.

"Well," he said, "at least you're with us again."

His voice sounded like a voice in an echo chamber. She stared up at him and his tall figure seemed to ripple slightly like a person seen in a distorted television tube. She closed her eyes and tried to clear her

95

thoughts. Then she opened them to stare up at him again. At least now he seemed to be standing there normally.

In a weak voice, she asked, "What happened to me?"

"You've had some kind of spell," he told her in that odd hollow voice. "You didn't report for work this morning and I came up to see what was wrong. You were here unconscious."

Alarm crossed her pretty face. "But how did you get in? I bolted the door after me. I always do."

His shrewd eyes showed disbelief. "Last night you didn't."

"But I'm sure of it," she insisted. "I was in your office and there was that angry scene between you and Madame Helene. You slapped her and she collapsed. I was certain she'd had a heart attack."

Dr. Martin Gill was staring at her. "You seem to remember all the details very clearly?"

"I do," she insisted. "I was upset and I came here to my apartment at once. I bolted the door and went to bed."

He was grimly studying her. "There was no scene downstairs," he said. "You must have had some kind of feverish dream."

"There was! You slapped Madame Helene!" she raised her voice in spite of her weakness.

He smiled coldly. "Does that sound like me?"

"I can't help it," she said wearily. "I saw it happen."

"Pure fantasy," he chided her. "In your illness you imagined it all."

96

"It's too real! I couldn't have!"

"You must have," he said in his suave fashion. "If you had really bolted the door I couldn't have gotten in here. At least not without breaking it down. And you can see I didn't do that."

CHAPTER SIX

Diana remained in bed for three days. Towards the evenings she would feel somewhat better and then there would come the long night with its dread dreams. She had frightening visions of the dead Walter Glendon in the room. Always the sad-faced poet would come to the foot of her bed, a gray wraith in the dark shadows, and attempt to tell her something. His lips would move but the words never came.

She also had another familiar dream. Madame Helene would come into the room and advance to the side of her bed and stand there glaring at her with her burning eyes. The white staring face of the old astrologer would show no expression and the thin lips with their slash of vivid lipstick never moved. The woman in the fantastic styles of forty and fifty years back made no attempt to communicate with her. She'd just watch her and then she would go.

On another night Diana experienced a variation of this nightmare. This time it was Dr. Martin Gill who entered her room and brought with him a half-dozen other men and women. He stood directly at the foot of her bed smiling at her in a sinister way while the others grouped around the sides. The whole picture was blurred and distorted but she knew they were in some way menacing her.

She lay there paralyzed with fear as she stared up into their smiling, twisted faces. They scarcely resembled humans to her. Even Dr. Martin Gill had subtly taken on a Satanic resemblance. They talked among themselves and nodded approvingly at her but she could not make out what they were saying. It was as if they were speaking in some foreign language. Just once did she catch a phrase from the lips of Dr. Martin Gill.

"She has been chosen," he intoned. "She has been chosen and she will not fail us."

Almost immediately the picture had faded from her mind and there was just a terrifying jumble of flight and confusion to replace it. She imagined she was fleeing from someone, racing down an endless dark street and never reaching safety. Never reaching anywhere! She opened her eyes with a small cry of fear and saw the cynical face of Dr. Martin Gill staring down at her.

"The weather has changed," he said. "It's raining out this morning and it's much cooler."

Diana stared up at him in troubled confusion. "I had those awful dreams again last night."

He smiled thinly. "I'm not surprised. You've been running high fevers. They are always more troublesome at night."

She frowned. "What has been wrong with me?"

"You picked up some kind of strange bug," he said with a bored look on his hawk face. "I've seen it happen before. You're feeling fine and a few hours later you're suddenly struck down and not able to function."

"How long before I'll feel better?" she asked anxiously.

"I'd say you are on the mend now. In fact I was going to suggest you get up for awhile. I'll have Anna come in to help you dress."

"No," she said in near panic as she rose on an elbow. "Not Anna. I don't want her around me."

His eyebrows raised. "She has been a good nurse to you during your illness. Do you think you can manage alone?"

"I'll take my time," she said, conscious of how weak she felt and what a terrifying experience leaving the comfort of her bed would be.

"I don't want you to overdo it," he said. "But I feel it is time you left your bed. One weakens in a surprisingly short time remaining in bed."

"I'll manage," she said.

The tall man smiled. "Perhaps I'll be seeing you downstairs. I'll be working in my office. And don't you worry about the magazine. I'll finish getting the November issue ready."

"There's only a little to do," she said. "If I can get downstairs I can do it myself."

"Just don't worry about it," he said. "I'll tell Anna to bring you up some breakfast on a tray. It will help build your strength."

Little as she liked seeing Anna in her room she didn't argue with him about this. She also hoped that some food would give her the energy she required so badly. As soon as the doctor left the room she made an effort to get out of bed. When she first stood on her feet using the bedpost for support the room swam around her. But she fought the dizziness and most of it vanished. Then she painfully made her way to the bathroom to wash and dress.

Cold water on her face helped. She found a simple blue linen dress and put it on. Then she sat limply before the dresser and tried to do something with her hair. It was straggly and unkempt. Her comb caught in mats continually and gave her a bad time. But eventually she looked better.

It was at this time that Anna arrived with her breakfast tray. The big swarthy woman said nothing but there was an air of triumph about her that let Diana know the peasant woman was enjoying her plight. Anna put down the tray and waddled out of the room without a word.

The breakfast was good and she felt better for it. In fact she was able to take proper stock of her position for the first time since her illness had hit her. She went to the window and looked out at the rain and the gray day. It was starting to look like fall.

What was she to do? The events of the night when she'd been taken ill had become mixed up in her mind. Her memory was really playing tricks on her. And she was suffering from a continual drowsiness and apathy. She knew she had planned to quit her job in the weird old mansion. But that no longer seemed too important. She'd get around to it later. The first thing was to regain her health again. She hoped it wouldn't take long now that she'd gotten over the worst of it.

The worst of what? She stood there frowning and watching the cars glide down the wet street outside her window. Dr. Martin Gill didn't seem to actually know what kind of virus she'd caught. At any rate it had been a nasty one. Her mind was left a shambles. She didn't seem to be able to organize herself.

She saw that there were some letters for her on the dresser. None of them had any importance except the one from Adam. In it he confirmed that he would be doing some traveling outside New York for the better part of a week. He said that he missed her and hoped she were all right. And he looked forward to their becoming engaged as soon as he returned. He ended the letter by asking her to get in touch with him by phone in any emergency and write regularly.

Diana wearily put the letter aside with the feeling of lassitude that had come to relax her making her feel there was no immediate need to reply to the letter. No point in worrying him about her illness she'd wait and write when she was herself again. This decided on she sat in the easy chair by the window for a half-hour and stared straight ahead of her as she tried to think out what she'd do next.

She came to the conclusion that the most important thing was to get the November issue of the magazine completed for the printers. And so she left her room, walking gingerly with her hand reached out to touch the wall now and then for support. She left the dark hall for the elevator cage and went downstairs. Again she traversed the shadows of the lower corridor to reach Dr. Martin Gill's office.

The door was closed and she knew that he must

have someone in for a private consultation. Doctor-governed-by-the-stars was the way he referred to himself. She wondered who he had in there with him. It took all her strength to reach her own office and she sank down behind her desk grateful to be there. Things seemed just about as she'd left them. She at once made an effort to resume her work.

The pages swam before her and she found it difficult to concentrate but she did get some work done. The dark day made her office really dingy so she switched on the lights and found they helped. She'd not been working long before the prim Miss Carlton appeared with her wire basket full of mail.

The gray-haired woman's stern face registered surprise as she looked in the door. "I didn't expect to see you down here. He said you were sick."

Diana looked up from the copy she was correcting with a wan smile. "I'm much better thanks."

"You don't look it," was Miss Carlton's frank opinion. "Your face is pale and you've got circles bigger than half-dollars under your eyes."

"I had quite a siege," she said.

Miss Carlton stared at her. "I had an idea you were going to leave."

"Oh?"

"I guess maybe you mentioned it," the gray-haired woman said. "And I wouldn't blame you. The girl that was here before Walter Glendon took the job didn't last long. The doctor and the old woman were too much for her. She called it the private asylum."

"I didn't know there had been someone else in this

job before Walter Glendon," Diana said. "Dr. Gill didn't mention it."

The woman with the mail basket in her hand looked wise. "You'd hardly expect him to. Not with that other girl running off the way she did. She was here one night when I went home. When I came back to work the next morning she'd left. That's the last I ever heard of her. Some mail came and he had me mark it 'not known' and send it back to the post office. After a while no more came." She rummaged in the basket. "Just three or four letters for editorial." She tossed them on her desk.

Diana took them and said, "You'll have to wait to take in the doctor's mail. He has someone in there with him."

"I know," Miss Carlton said pulling a long face. "One of those hippies. I don't understand why he wastes time on the likes of them." And she went out and headed back to her own cubicle at the front of the building.

Diana sat back in her chair and stared at the mail with a slight frown. So she was the third person to have accepted the position of editor of the astrology magazine. One of them had died and the other had vanished. What was likely to happen to her? It seemed odd that Dr. Gill hadn't mentioned the girl who had been in charge of this office before Walter Glendon? And why had she made such a sudden decision to leave?

Had she found something out? Something of so terrifying a nature that she couldn't dare remain in the grim old house any longer? And where had she vanished? Dr. Martin Gill apparently didn't know or pretended not to. He had refused to give any forwarding address for her mail. It was a mystery. And her head was in no shape to cope with mysteries. Sighing she returned to her task.

She was giving her attention to the several letters that had arrived. They were all of a general nature. One was a letter asking for a reprint of an article that had appeared in a previous issue. The others wanted information on where to get various out-of-print astrological works. She was reading the last of these when she heard the voice of Dr. Martin Gill and a younger man in the hall.

A moment later the two strolled by her door. She had only a passing glimpse of them but she at once identified the youth with the black-rimmed glasses, long blond hair to his shoulders and a prominent nose crowning a stern young face as being the same young man she'd seen attending the group session the night she'd looked after the front door.

The two passed on along the hall as the doctor saw him out. He returned a few minutes later with a look of satisfaction on his hawk face. "It's good to see you able to work again," he said.

"I'm not doing too much," she warned him.

"Nor should you the first day," he said.

"The November issue is almost complete," she told him. "I have a query here concerning cusps which should be answered in a short article. I'd like to do it but I'm not sure I know enough about it."

He at once showed interest. "I'll explain. The lines dividing the houses of a horoscope chart are the house

105

cusps. The Ascendant marks the first house cusp. The next angular line is the second house cusp, and so on. In the zodiac the first degree of Aries marks the first sign cusp. The first degree of Taurus is the mark of the second sign cusp, and so on around the wheel."

She listened, trying to concentrate in spite of her dulled state of mind. "I think I understand. The confusion occurs for people who are born on or very near a sign cusp. They don't know which birth sign to take?"

"Exactly," he said. "Too many astrologers confuse these people. The proper principle is simple enough. The best thing to do in the case of cuspal births is to adopt the sign of the house approaching. A person born November 22nd, for instance, could be either Scorpio or Sagittarius. Such a person is usually safer to adopt the oncoming house, or Sagittarius in this case. And this is especially true if Mercury happens to be in the oncoming sign, which it often is, for this planet is never farther from the sun than twenty-eight degrees."

"That makes it clear enough," she said. "I think I can work something up from that."

"You mustn't work too late today," he warned.

"I won't," she said. "When Miss Carlson brought the mail she happened to mention you had someone here as editor before Walter Glendon. A girl who vanished suddenly."

Dr. Martin Gill at once lost his look of good humor. "Miss Carlton talks far too much and makes little sense most of the time as you must have observed."

"I'm sorry," she said. "I only mentioned it because I wondered what had happened. Why she hadn't been

106

able to cope with the work? I thought the answer might be beneficial to me."

He gave a deep sigh. "It was one of those things. I took the girl on because she claimed editorial experience. After a few days it was revealed she had none. I gave her a lecture and she walked out."

"I see," Diana said quietly. "It was a question of incompetence."

He was frowning. "That and nothing more. What did Miss Carlton suggest?"

Diana hesitated, not wanting to get the prim woman in any more trouble than she had already. She said, "I don't think she suggested anything beyond saying she left very suddenly."

"She did. And now you know why."

"I can see that it would be awkward," she agreed, wanting to placate him. His explanation of the affair sounded reasonable. Another bout of weariness had come to her again and she simply didn't have the energy to worry it out.

"I'm going up to have my usual afternoon sherry with Madame Helene at four-thirty," the tall man said. "I think it would do you good to stop work then and join us. We usually screen a film and it's amusing and bound to relax you."

Her impulse was to refuse him but that would probably only put him in a mood again. Not wanting any more tension, she said, "If you're sure Madame Helene won't think I'm intruding."

"She'd be glad to have you. She enjoys company when she's at herself."

Diana worked on at a slow pace and finished the

short article before Dr. Gill returned to the office to escort her upstairs for the weird afternoon entertainment session. Dr. Martin Gill, perfectly tailored in a dark suit, looked pleased with himself as they went up in the elevator.

"Are you familiar with the silent films, Diana?" he asked.

"Only classics such as the Chaplin comedies. I've seen a few others on television."

His hypnotic eyes fixed on hers. "Silent film was the greatest form of screen art," he said earnestly. "With all the improvements in cameras, film stock and techniques the moderns have never matched the work of the early masters."

"Madame Helene mentioned D. W. Griffith to me," she said.

He smiled bleakly. "She was an intimate of David Wark Griffith. His fortunes might have been much different if he'd taken her advice. But Griffith had no faith in the stars and wouldn't listen to her. As a result he died in comparative obscurity."

The old elevator came to a creaking halt. She said, "Yet his work still lives."

"Of course, he was one of the greatest," he said, opening the gate and letting her go out first. "But he could have accomplished much more if he'd not turned his back on astrology."

They entered the vast living room of the upper floor apartment and she found it even more archaic and depressing during the day time. As they walked the length of the room she spied the stretched-out figure of Madame Helene on the chaise lounge. When she and

Dr. Martin Gill went up on the small stage the ancient astrologer sat up stiffly and stared at them.

"Why is she here?" Madame Helene asked the doctor abruptly as if Diana couldn't hear her.

Dr. Martin Gill looked slightly embarrassed. "Diana has come at my invitation. You'll remember we discussed this and I suggested it was advisable for her to see some of the old films."

The mask-like white face of Madame Helene showed just a hint of petulance. "I don't remember ever talking about it."

"You've forgotten as you so often do," he told her in a placating tone.

"I don't want her here with us," the astrologer said in the old woman's voice that didn't match the restored beauty of her face.

"You don't mean that," Dr. Gill said treating her like a child.

Diana felt she should speak up and offer him a release from the humiliating predicament. She said, "I'd just as soon go to my apartment. I don't feel too well."

"No," the tall man said sternly. "I insist that you remain. I'll get you and the Madame some sherry. Then I'll pull down the screen and get the projector ready." He left them for a moment.

Diana stood awkwardly by the chaise lounge. "I don't mean to force myself on you," she told the old woman.

Madame Helene stared straight ahead of her, seemingly in deep despair. "It is what he wants. And I always have to do as he wants."

"Not in this case. I'll go."

"No," the old woman said quickly with surprising vigor. "That wouldn't solve anything at all."

By this time he had returned with a glass of sherry in each hand and gave it to them. He smiled at Diana. "It will take me a few minutes to get everything set up. The screen is on the wall by the door we came in. And the projector is in a tiny booth behind this stage. If you look you can see the opening in the wall for the projection lens."

She looked up and saw the tiny square in the rear wall above the stage. She said, "It's a very professional arrangement. You must screen many films."

He smiled wisely. "We knew we would be and that's why we had the booth and equipment installed when we came here."

Madame Helene studied her over her glass of sherry. "Do you like the movies?"

"Very much," she said.

Dr. Martin Gill smiled. "Tonight we'll be showing a silent one. Vintage of the late 1920s. It's a murder mystery. I think you'll like it." And he left them to go out a door at the corner of the stage that she decided must lead to the projection booth.

Diana sat on a chair which the doctor had put out near the chaise lounge for her. It was odd to be on the stage overlooking the big room. She tried to imagine what it must be like when Madame Helene addressed her astrology study groups from up there.

"Do you think murder is ever justified?" The surprising question came from Madame Helene.

She at once supposed the subject had come up because of the mystery film they were about to watch.

With a wry smile, she said, "I've never given it a great deal of thought."

The eyes in the mask-like pale face of the old woman were boring into her. "There are times when to murder is to dispense justice," Madame Helene said in her quavering voice.

Diana stared at the weird figure seated on the chaise lounge and once again was certain the ancient astrologer was mad. She said, "That could be dangerous thinking. Not all of us are qualified to dispense justice."

"You can't depend on the law," Madame Helene said. "The law cheats us. You must act for yourself. Act as you see fit."

"But that is against the protection of the community," Diana argued quietly. "The law is designed to protect the group."

"And deny the individual," the old woman said. "Some must rise above the law. Risk all for their beliefs."

It wasn't a point Diana wished to discuss and so she was glad when the lights in the big room were turned off and the film began. The screen at the other end of the room was a good-sized one and the picture was sharp and clear. The hum of the projector could be clearly heard from the booth as the film was silent. The credits showed names unknown to her and the movie began in a London setting revealing vintage cars and quaint female fashions like the dresses worn by Madame Helene.

The story wasn't too interesting. Titles flashed on between dramatic scenes to furnish the dialogue. It

111

would have been amusing if the old woman on the chaise lounge had not been taking it so seriously. The beam of light from the booth to the screen allowed Diana to study Madame Helene in the near darkness. And the old astrologer was plainly following the action of the movie with frantic excitement.

Her thin body leaned forward in moments of dramatic action and she would gasp and let out cries of encouragement when the hero was besting the villains. Through other scenes the old woman kept up a constant mumbling and never let those mad eyes leave the screen. It was a fantastic performance.

Once again Diana was experiencing a headache. She'd finished her sherry and was trying to keep her attention on the movie. But it was too preposterous to really interest her. And then suddenly she saw a familiar face on the screen. The face of Madame Helene, though she must have played the role nearly forty years before, her features were recognizable. So were the black, staring eyes. And the face on the screen had the mask-like look of Madame Helene in the present. No doubt make-up explained the oddness of her appearance then and her many face-lifts had brought the look in real life.

Madame Helene was playing the part of the villain's secretary in the story. She had little to do but stare at him behind his back and hold a pencil and pad in hand. When he turned to her she registered fear. And that was about it. Her presence in the film was of extremely short duration. But the old woman on the chaise lounge was literally in an ecstasy over her performance on the screen.

112

When the movie came to an end and the lights came on again Madame Helene turned to her. "You saw me, didn't you?"

"Yes. It came as a surprise. I didn't realize you were an actress."

"I was a great star," the old woman said proudly. This seemed sad in view of the bit part she'd played.

"What was your screen name?" Diana asked, thinking a polite interest was necessary.

However, the reaction on the aged astrologer's part was unexpected. Madame Helene glared at her. "What difference does that make to you?"

Startled, she said, "None."

"Then mind your own business," the old woman said angrily. And she called out, "Martin!" in a loud quavering voice.

The tall, bald man rejoined them with a questioning expression on his lined face. "Did I hear you calling me, Madame?"

Madame Helene nodded indignantly. "Yes. She was asking me a lot of questions. Wanting to know my screen name!"

The doctor turned to Diana with a slight smile. "Madame is very jealous of her privacy. She prefers her film career to be part of a secret past. I'm sure you'll understand."

"Of course," Diana said.

Madame Helene was looking up at the tall doctor. "I was good today, wasn't I, Martin?"

"Excellent," he said suavely. "It's one of your best roles."

"I was good in all of them," the thin old woman on

113

the chaise lounge said, her mottled hands folded in her lap. "I scaled the heights."

Diana saw it all as a tragic comedy. Dr. Martin Gill was clearly catering to Madame Helene in showing her old movies over and over again. Keeping the old woman happy in the present so he could manipulate her as head of the astrological group which he controlled.

"Diana and I have to leave you now," the doctor told the old woman gently.

The mad eyes in the white face gazed up at him imploringly. "But you will come back?"

The doctor took one of the mottled hands in his and patted it ever so tenderly. "Don't I always?" Then he kissed the old woman on the cheek.

As he and Diana were going out the enormous Anna came waddling into the room. She nodded to the doctor and glared at Diana. Then she went on up to join Madame Helene. No doubt she was there to take her to another area of the apartment for her evening meal.

Dr. Martin Gill held open the gate of the elevator for Diana to enter first. He said, "I hope you weren't bored."

"Only a little," she said. "Seeing Madame Helene in the film sparked my interest."

He gave her a strange look as he set the elevator in motion. Turning directly to her, he said, "That wasn't Madame Helene on the screen. It was a look-alike. She enjoys believing she was an actress and I encourage it."

114

She frowned. "But the woman playing the secretary role looked exactly like her."

"I know," he said. "She was a minor actress of that era who resembled Madame Helene a great deal. I've collected most of the old films she appeared in and the Madame gets a great deal of pleasure from them."

"Isn't it wrong to deceive her?"

He shook his head as the elevator halted at the second floor. "No. She is old and ill. It's a kindness. You'll want to be getting off here."

"Thank you," she said. And she left the elevator while he remained in it to continue down to the ground floor.

She let herself into her apartment in a puzzled state of mind. The experience upstairs had been a strange one. The old woman watching the ancient movie was actually living more in the shadow life of the screen than she was in the present. It was as if she'd already become one of those ghostly figures who lived only as flickering images in a darkened room.

Diana also felt certain the woman she'd seen on the screen had been Madame Helene. Yet Dr. Martin Gill had taken great pains to deny it. What reason could he have for doing this?

CHAPTER SEVEN

As the days went by the thing that bothered Diana the most was her total lack of initiative. She seemed completely unable to make decisions and carry them out. Her odd headaches also continued seeming worst in the morning. And if the headaches were a problem the dreams that she blamed for causing them were even more disturbing.

She had them every night now. It seemed she hardly closed her eyes before the phantoms pursued her. The unhappy Walter Glendon always played a role in the fantastic dramas of her nightmares. But there were other, and more real figures, who stalked through the tormented corridors of her sleeping mind.

Dr. Martin Gill frequently appeared to stand by her bed and study her with smug satisfaction. Others came with him. Faces she had never seen before peered down at her as she stared up at them from her pillow with terrified eyes. This one dream never lasted too long. But it was always a terrifying ordeal.

She had other dreams in which she was a frantic participant. In one of them she was driving in a car with Dr. Martin Gill. It was a convertible with the top down and they were going at a breath-taking speed. Down the broad expressway the car careened. And as its speed increased it swayed wildly with screeching tires whenever they approached a turn. Until finally on one turn the car went out of control altogether. She saw the hapless expression on Dr. Martin Gill's hawk face as he fought to avoid an accident.

But it was no use. The convertible bounced over the center lane into the path of an oncoming truck. She screamed out her fear just before the truck crashed into them and everything dwindled into nothingness. This nightmare would be swiftly followed by another in which Dr. Martin Gill was pursuing her through the dark corridors of the house with a gun in his hand. She kept eluding him but somehow he always managed to catch up with her.

The dreams seemed to be accompanied by a difficulty in breathing. She would toss restlessly in bed feeling she could not breathe. As if she were smothering. Beads of perspiration would break out at her temples and she would wake frightened and confused. Somewhere at the back of her mind a small voice warned her that she was remaining too long at the old house on Beacon Street. That it was a scene of sinister happenings. And somehow she had been caught up in the evil.

Still she had no will to leave. She no longer thought about going out of the house. She was working on the January issue of the magazine and doing the things that Dr. Martin Gill ordered her. And she was naively pleased whenever he complimented her. But her personal affairs were being neglected. She knew it, yet didn't care.

In her spare time she kept the apartment neat and clean. She read little though she sometimes watched the television in the library on the ground floor. Often she would just sit and stare out her window at the nearby Public Gardens. Meanwhile the letters that came to her from Adam Purcell in New York remained unanswered. It seemed too much bother to write.

One afternoon when she was working in her office she received a phone call from the troubled young man. As soon as the long distance operator put him through, he demanded, "What's happened to you, Diana?"

"Nothing," she said.

"I haven't had any letters from you," he complained.

"I was ill for a few days," she said tonelessly.

"Are you better now?"

"Yes. It was nothing serious."

"Then you should have written me," he worried. "I've been frantic to hear you. Thinking all sorts of things. What's wrong?"

"I've been very busy. There was a lot of work to do to bring the magazine up-to-date."

At the New York end of the line Adam sounded concerned. "You might have let me know. Somehow your voice seems different. Sort of lifeless. Are you weak after your sickness?"

"I suppose so," she said. That small voice at the back of her mind urged her to tell him that she was

118

continually frightened, caught in a weird sort of prison, and without a normal desire to save herself. She knew she should be asking for help and yet she wasn't. She couldn't summon the energy.

"I'm going to try and get a few days off and see you," he promised. "I may manage it in a week or two."

"Don't bother on my account," she found herself saying. It was like listening to another person speaking words that had been set out for her on some idiot card like the kind they used for prompting in television. She was behaving in this strange way and she didn't know why. The overwhelming reason seemed to be she didn't want any arguments. Anything was better than having arguments!

Adam was hurt. "You talk as if you don't care whether you see me again or not!"

"I'm doing my job the same as you're doing yours," she told him. "I don't think you have any right to call me with a lot of nagging talk. I don't want to be nagged!" Her head was beginning to ache again and she was near tears. The voice begging her to appeal for help before it was too late was bringing inner turmoil to her.

"If that's the way you feel I won't call you again," Adam said in a taut voice. "If you need me you know where to reach me. I hope you'll think about this and realize you've not been very pleasant." And he hung up.

She put down the phone with consternation shadowing her lovely face. What insanity had she committed? Adam had been on the line ready and anxious to help her and she'd coldly refused his aid. Tears brimmed in her eyes as she tried to understand why she'd acted as she had. It was the thought of conflict that she hadn't been able to bear. Adam entering the picture would have meant a violent confrontation with the people in the old house. A confrontation she wasn't in the mood to endure.

She went back to work and soon forgot about the call. If you didn't upset yourself too much about such things your memory quickly erased them. That was what she'd recently discovered. Days took on a same pleasant shade of gray. No highlights and no let downs. If only those terrifying dreams that plagued her nights would end and that tormenting inner voice would stop trying to alarm her!

Often when she became weary at her desk she would go out and chat with the prim Miss Carlton for a moment. It seemed to her that lately the gray-haired woman who worked at the house from nine to five had grown more careful in what she said.

As she entered the office the receptionist was reading the Boston tabloid paper. She had it open in such a way that Diana could see the large photos on the front page and read the headline. In large black type the paper proclaimed: "PUBLIC GARDEN RIOT!" And under the blaring headline was a head and shoulders photo of a man named as instigator of the outbreak. Her eyes opened wide for she recognized him at once as the youthful, long-haired, hippie who had attended the group meeting one night. She'd also seen him on a later occasion coming out of Dr. Martin Gill's private office.

120

Touching the paper, she exclaimed, "I know him! He's been here!"

Miss Carlton gave her the dubious glance she seemed to have for everyone in the old mansion. She then folded the paper closed to study the photo for herself. "Are you sure?"

Diana nodded excitedly. "Yes. He's too much a type to forget."

"Hippies all look alike to me!" The prim woman sniffed.

"Not to me they don't," Diana insisted. "I'd remember that face anywhere. I saw him twice in this house."

Miss Carlton looked grim as she studied the front page. "Well, it seems he's in plenty of trouble now."

"When was the riot?" she asked.

"Yesterday," Miss Carlton said, giving her an odd look. "Sunday! You surely haven't lost rack of the days."

She had but she didn't want the gray-haired woman to realize it. So she said, "Of course it had to be yesterday. You don't come in on Sundays."

"Saturdays are my off days as well," the older woman reminded her.

"I know."

Miss Carlton frowned. "You've been looking peaked lately. I'd say you've been working too hard and don't get out enough."

"I'm fine," she said, embarrassed. She was doubly uneasy because that tiny inner voice was raising a rumpus again. Daring her to tell the truth! Urging her to ask Miss Carlton for help! But she fought against listening to it.

"You've lasted longer than I expected," the prim woman said. "There was a time before you had that sick spell I guessed you were ready to leave right away."

"I thought it over."

Miss Carlton nodded. "I know how it is. I've promised myself to find me a job where the working conditions are more pleasant. But I never do. The minute I get home I have so many things to look after. I have a widower brother and his two grown sons to keep house for."

"That must be hard work," Diana said, though she really wasn't paying much attention to the conversation. She was thinking of that hippie and wondering why it all seemed so important to her. Then she suddenly remembered. In one of her newspaper columns Madame Helene had predicted the riot. And on a Sunday! And it had taken place on a Sunday!

Excitedly, she said, "May I have the paper for a few minutes?"

"Take it," Miss Carlton said with a bewildered look. "I'm finished with it anyway."

Diana took the tabloid with a smile. "Thanks. I want to show it to Dr. Gill. I'm positive he'll be interested."

"Don't count on it," was the older woman's advice. "You never can tell about him."

Diana waited no longer but left the tiny office to hurry down the hall and find Dr. Martin Gill. The hawk-faced man was at his desk reading some sort of report when she rushed in. He raised his eyes to her with a polite smile of inquiry.

122

"My! You seem very excited," he said.

"I am," she told him. And going over to the desk held the paper out for him. "Did you see this?"

He took it. "Yes," he said, studying the front page with a satisfied smile. "I think it's about time the police clamped down on such hippie demonstrations. You have to begin somewhere."

"I wasn't thinking of that," she said. "Don't you recognize the young man they arrested for starting it?"

Dr. Martin Gill smiled in his casual way. "I can't say that I do."

She was taken back. "But you must!"

"I don't."

"He was here to your group astrology session. I saw him. He was wearing a black leather jacket."

"I don't place him," the doctor contended.

"You must," she said. "He came back later in the daytime. I saw you two leaving your private office."

His manner was one of innocence. "No," he said. "Not that young man. I have given private consultations to several hippie characters and it is true we have some attend the group meetings but I don't recall this face. Or his name for that matter."

Diana stared at him. "But I saw him with you."

The tall doctor rose from his chair and came over beside her. He placed an arm gently around her, "I say you've made a mistake."

Her gaze was bewildered. "So much like him," she murmured. "Even the same coloring."

"It's a natural error," Dr. Martin Gill said suavely, "the kind anyone could have made."

123

She sighed. "I suppose so."

"Don't worry about it," he said.

She stared at the paper as it rested on his desk. The face of the arrested man was still face upward to her. She said, "That's the riot Madame Helene predicted. You remember?"

"Indeed I do," he said, in good humor again. "I've had a number of phone calls complimenting us. And I'm seeing mention of it is made on television and in the papers tomorrow. We can't miss an excellent opportunity for publicity like this."

"How could she know?" Diana asked.

"Second sight or whatever you wish to call it," he said. "She may be old and slipping mentally but at times she has positively brilliant flashes. This was one of them."

Diana gave him a searching look. "Couldn't it have been just chance?"

"There was nothing of chance involved," he said sternly. "You shouldn't be so skeptical in the face of genius."

She considered. "This prediction coming true will add to her followers. People will be flocking to buy her charts."

Dr. Martin Gill, resplendent in a pearl gray suit and matching accessories, moved away from her and began to pace up and down the carpeted office floor. "I certainly hope that is what happens," he said.

"It must help whenever one of her predictions comes true."

He nodded as he continued to pace. "We found that out when the prediction of Governor Denton's assassination proved correct. Coming right after the Kennedy assassinations made it all the more sensational. And the Madame did give a warning about JFK, though she missed out on Bobby."

Diana was standing there in a stunned state. Inside her there was the familiar turmoil again. That nagging voice was demanding that she tell him he'd lied to her. That the young man pictured in the tabloid had been the one she'd seen twice in the house. But she didn't want the argument and scene that would follow such a declaration. So she silenced the voice though the effort of it was making her feel ill.

In a dull tone, she asked, "How can a person like Madame Helene know such things? Be able to predict them so correctly?"

The doctor paused in his pacing with the avid look of a top salesman on his hawk face. "The Madame is poised between this world and the next. With great age there comes a feeling for that other realm. And she is more than a century old. She's walking in the valley of death and she hears voices that can't reach us."

She frowned. "You almost make her sound like a ghost!"

"In a way she is," he went on quickly, caught up by his own enthusiasm. "A living ghost able to tell us things we would otherwise never know. She proved that when she told Julia James the very day on which she'd die. Julia wouldn't listen to her and she is on that other side now."

"I don't like it," Diana murmured in her new tone-less voice. "It's not healthy!"

"Nonsense," he said sharply, his manner changing in a second as it so often did. He stood there in the middle of the gloomy office with his tall body slightly crouched as he leaned toward her. "Don't ever let me hear you say that again!"

She closed her eyes. Her head was throbbing. She couldn't face the scene that would follow if she went against him. In a small voice she said, "I'm sorry."

"You should be," Dr. Martin Gill said sternly. "You are part of this organization now. You must learn to be loyal above all else. I will not brook disloyalty among my staff."

"I meant no harm," she said. She was sorry she'd ever ventured into the room with the paper. She wished devoutly she'd remained in the calm of her office. This was what she got for involving herself. She'd know better another time. Anything for quiet! Anything to ease that throbbing head!

"Madame Helene is a wonderful woman," he said with emphasis, his burning hypnotic eyes fixed on hers. "She is doing a great work. And this work is going to bring tremendous results for all of us. Have you any idea of how powerful we are becoming?"

She shook her head. "No."

Dr. Martin Gill straightened his shoulders and a greedy smile appeared on his hawk face. "We are on our way to being one of the most wealthy organizations in the mass astrology field. And the faithful are lining up behind us. They like the touch of ESP and spiritualism we're adding to our basic astrological line. One day we'll be a power in this nation."

Diana stared at him. "Is that what you want? Power?"

"Let's not forget the money," he said with a knowing wink. "It's a combination that goes well together. Put aside your foolish notions of what is right and wrong about our work. Concentrate on helping us become more successful. There's nothing I wouldn't do to make Madame Helene truly famous now."

"What good will it do her?" Diana asked. "She's too old and she's so lost in the past."

"She will become a symbol," the tall, thin man said in almost rapture. "And don't forget she chose you to be one of us. You were selected to join our cause by her."

"By her?" Diana asked. "Surely she had some help from you."

He smiled complacently. "I'll not deny I have a part in all the decisions made by Madame Helene. But you must accept what I'm telling you as truth."

Had it not been for the new apathy which was dominating her she would have protested against his words. But there was little left to her but a dull curiosity. She wanted to learn the truth even though she knew she wasn't likely to do anything about it.

She said, "It's your dream. Your empire. You are using her only as a name to build it on."

"Why shouldn't I?" he asked, almost harshly. "It

is my brain and will that has made Madame Helene the world figure she is. When I first discovered her she was a nothing!"

"Even with her gift of prophecy?" Something in her could not resist this mocking comment. Her personality had not been completely quenched.

Dr. Martin Gill frowned. "Her gift for prophecy came later. Developed largely through my coaching. I have given her the position she has today and even when she is gone this organization will live."

"Without a prophet?"

His expression was grim. "A new prophet will arise. Let me show you how widely our voice has spread," he said. And he went over to the wall safe.

She watched carefully as he manipulated the combination and then pulled down the handle to swing open the heavy steel door of the walk-in safe. He walked inside and vanished for a moment. While she waited she allowed her eyes to once again take in the rows of smiling autographed photos on the wall. The mocking faces of the Hollywood ghosts!

Dr. Martin Gill emerged from the safe with a folder in his hands. A triumphant smile showed on his hawk face. His penetrating eyes gleamed with greedy delight as he came over to her. "I can show you this file because I can trust you," he said. "This is our master list of those affiliated with Madame Helene Astrological Service all over the world. If I told you how many thousand names there were in here you wouldn't believe it."

"Surely the organization has grown large enough," she said.

"Not yet," was his reply, as he closed the file. "Nor have we attained our goals in other directions. The Madame will continue her prophecies and her power will increase. This prediction about the riot in the Public Gardens yesterday was only minor. But look at the publicity it has brought us and will continue to bring us."

She excused herself after a moment and left him taking the file of members over to his desk to study with the wall safe still open. She knew that all the important documents and records were kept in there. And she suspected he might keep large amounts of cash there as well. Her talk with him left her more convinced than ever that he had a fanatical ambition to spread the gospel of Madame Helene. And that he would not be too scrupulous as to how he accomplished it.

Taking the elevator to the second floor she wearily made her way to her apartment. In the dim recesses of her mind she still believed she had seen the hippie in the house. And Dr. Martin Gill's emphatic denial of this made her suspicious that the young man might have deliberately staged the riot to make Madame Helene's prediction come true. And this led to the frightening thought that other events might have been arranged in the same way. The assassination of Governor Denton for instance or the tragic accident that took singing star, Julia James' life!

Diana was standing staring at herself in her dresser mirror as these terrifying possibilities came to her. Her face reflected the horror of her thoughts. And she was shocked to see how wan and exhausted she looked.

She raised her hands to cover her face and turned away from the mirror trying to fight back the panic rising in her. Somehow she must hold on!

Taking a deep breath she lowered her hands and walked slowly towards her bed. She needed a rest. That was why she felt so badly and had such wild fancies. It was ridiculous to believe that the Madame Helene organization would arrange a riot, an assassination or a fatal accident for their purposes. No one would ever take such a story seriously. The old woman had been lucky and careful to make fairly vague predictions in most cases that could be twisted into matching certain happenings when they occurred.

Forcing herself to think this way she again quieted that small voice of her integrity which urged her to face the evil in the old house with realism. To seek escape first and then help. She sighed as she prepared to stretch out on the bed. And then her eyes opened wide and her mouth gaped as she stumbled back in dismay. For there in the middle of her bed lay a tiny dead mouse and tied around its neck, as if throttle it, was a twisted skein of hairs from her head!

With a small sob finally escaping from her lips she turned away from the disgusting sight and hurried across to the door. When she opened it to go out into the hallway she was confronted by the weird figure of Madame Helene standing out there.

The ancient astrologer was wearing some kind of silver gown with black velvet trim. The evening gown revealed her thin shoulders and she wore a beaded band around her mass of upswept dyed black hair. Her pale, staring mask of a face regarded Diana blankly. But her mad eyes gleamed with hatred.

"You are too ambitious!" she accused Diana.

Diana was too upset to think clearly. But she managed, "What are you doing standing out there?"

Madame Helene lifted her head arrogantly. "I ask the questions here. You answer them."

"Not all of them," she said desperately. And turning to point at the bed, she asked, "Were you spying on me because you and that crazy Anna put that thing there?"

"You seem terribly afraid," the old woman said in her quavering voice, not denying she had a part in the distasteful act.

She turned on the old astrologer in a rage. "You and Anna are working your black magic on me!" she accused her. "You're trying to destroy me!"

"The stars are against you," Madame Helene said with crazy dignity. "You are a Gemini influenced by Pisces and Leo. And because of this you are doomed!" And having delivered this sepulchral oration the old woman turned and walked off into the shadows.

Diana stood there staring after her. There was no question that in her mad way the astrologer hated her. She tolerated her only because Dr. Martin Gill pressured her into it. And so by way of revenge Madame Helene must have had Anna carefully collect hair combings from the wastebasket in the apartment and arrange this bizarre black magic token.

Still sick with shock Diana took the creaking elevator downstairs and went directly to the office of the doctor. He was in the act of closing the wall safe door when she entered. And again she noticed that he had to take particular care to see it securely closed. When it clicked shut he turned to her.

"Back so soon?" he asked.

She stood there accusingly, feeling as if her body were swaying. She said, "How did Anna get into my apartment?"

The tall, bald man stared at her. "Why do you ask that?"

"I want to know."

"I don't think she can get into your apartment," he said rather lamely.

"She must have a key!" Diana insisted.

Dr. Martin Gill was frowning as he came closer to her. "I wish you'd stop these dramatic questions and explain yourself."

Diana gave him a bitter smile. "I'd rather you come to my room and see for yourself."

"All right, I will," he said.

They made no attempt at conversation during the short trip to the second floor in the elevator. She led him along the hall and through the doorway of the apartment. In her haste she'd left the door open. She walked to the side of the bed and was about to point out the weird token when she saw that it was gone.

He said, "Well?"

She turned to look into his bland face with an air of confusion. "There was a filthy black magic token on my bed. They've taken it when I was downstairs."

"They?"

"Anna and Madame Helene. Madame Helene was

132

standing outside my door when I found it. I'm sure she stationed herself there to discover my reaction."

Dr. Martin Gill's lean face revealed interest. "What sort of thing was it?"

"A dead mouse with a twisted rope made of my hair tied around its neck. It was bound to have some meaning as an evil charm."

"How do you know it was your hair?"

"It had to be mine," she insisted. "It matched the color of my hair exactly. And the only way Anna could get it was to come in here and steal combings from my wastebasket. Just as she came in and left that wretched thing on my bed."

"I see," he said. "Well, I don't think Anna has a key. But this is a serious business. I'll surely look into it."

Diana was certain he never would.

CHAPTER EIGHT

And then a day or two later there came a new and more shattering complication. Diana found herself standing on busy Tremont Street across from the white-steepled Park Street Church. The bells of the church were pealing out the noon hour on the warm September day and it was their sound that must have brought her to full consciousness.

She stood there trying to remember. People bustled by, some staring at her and others not noticing her at all. She was dressed in a yellow suit and carrying a matching handbag. Apparently she'd carefully selected them for this outing. But she had no memory of doing it or even of leaving the old house on Beacon Street. The whole thing was a blank in her mind.

As she stood there staring across at the subway station she could recall sitting down to breakfast. And then everything was a blur in her mind. Now it was hours later and she was standing confused in the middle of a busy street. Why had she left the old house? What was she doing here? Where had she been?

These were questions that terrified her and made her feel certain she must be losing her mind. First the awful dreams followed by those sickening headaches and now this worst experience of all. She'd certainly had a blackout of memory and it might be only the beginning of a series of such attacks. The palms of her hand were wet with sweat as she nervously twisted the strap of her handbag and considered what she should do.

She was ill. She had to be to suffer an experience such as this. But what was the nature of her illness? Perhaps a spell cast on her by the malevolent Anna and the weird Madame Helene. The two surely were strange enough to indulge in black magic. And she knew they hated her.

The lights changed and she decided to cross the street and walk through the Common to Beacon Street and then gradually find her way back to the old house. She could think of nowhere else to go. She had come to depend on Gill. And he was a medical doctor. Or so he claimed.

She was relieved to have the rush of the busy Tremont Street behind her. Moving past the subway entrance she began strolling up a tree-lined walk that led in the direction of Beacon Street. On this pleasant day there were many people seated on the benches set out at intervals. She halted once to look back at the stores of Tremont Street and the heavy traffic. Then she turned and began her journey to the series of steps, dedicated to soldiers of the First World War, that led to the Beacon Street level.

All the while she walked that inner voice nagged at her. It warned her she was making a mistake. That instead of returning to the strange old mansion she

135

should seek out a policeman and tell him her story. Ask to be sent to a hospital. She fought to still the voice by thinking that this wouldn't help. The police would consider her mad. And the suave Dr. Martin Gill would be able to prove her wrong in any charges she made against him. Depend on that!

Still the struggle between her apathy and this inner warning voice went on. But she still headed for Beacon Street and the familiar four-storied brick house with the gray trim. She was almost eager to get back. The crowds frightened her and the sun made her headache worse. And above all she was terrified that another blackout might come upon her and she'd wander madly through the streets until some dreadful fate overtook her.

She pushed herself on at a faster pace. It was ironic that while the voice of warning nagged at her to look elsewhere for aid, she kept heading back to the headquarters of Madame Helene. When she arrived at the door she rang the bell impatiently and trembled as she waited.

The prim Miss Carlton opened the door for her. "Where have you been?" the older woman asked.

"In the Common," she said.

"You're dressed to the nines," the older woman said. "The sun should have been good for you."

Diana stepped inside grateful for the coolness and shadow of the hall. "It's still very warm," she said.

"You'd never know it in here," Miss Carlton said in her no-nonsense fashion as she started back to her tiny office.

136

"Has Dr. Gill returned from the Washington Street offices?" she asked the older woman.

Miss Carlton shook her head. "He's not going until later today. He's still here."

She felt a deep relief. "I'm glad to hear that," she said.

The gray-haired woman gave her a bleak glance. "I'd like to have your kind of job. Be able to dress up and take off whenever I felt like it. But no such luck. I'm stuck here in this two-by-four closet they call a reception office."

Diana made no reply to this but went on down the dark hall to see Dr. Martin Gill. She couldn't wait to talk to him and tell him what had happened to her. Ask for some explanation. As it turned out she almost ran into him in the hallway as he emerged from her office.

He studied her in surprise. "I've been looking for you."

She swallowed hard. "Yes. I can imagine."

The tall man stared at her. "You look very attractive in that yellow outfit. Where have you been?"

"That's a long story," she said.

The hawk-faced man smiled thinly. "Perhaps you'd better come into my office and sit down while you tell it to me."

She did as he asked. Seated across the desk from him she told her story. Ending with a plaintive, "I don't understand any of it. Why I went out or where I went? As soon as I recovered from the blackout I came straight back here."

His hypnotic eyes were fixed on her. "You were wise in that," he said. "If another attack hit you it's hard to say where you might have wound up."

"I thought about that," she agreed forlornly.

"This must be an aftermath of your illness," he went on. "I'm afraid we've let you work too hard."

"I don't mind the work. I like it."

"But you overdo."

"I haven't noticed," she said. And then looking embarrassed she added, "I've been starting to think perhaps Anna's spell against me is working."

He frowned. "That's childish."

"I'm frightened," she said simply as if that were sufficient reason for her theory.

"You're much too intelligent to believe in Anna's peasant evil. It's merely a question of an overwrought nervous system. I doubt if what happened today will ever happen again."

"I sincerely hope not," she said. "It's your opinion as a medical man that I'm merely over-tired?"

"Correct," he said.

"I came out of it in the midst of the noon-hour rush on Tremont Street," she said with a tiny shudder. "I don't want to go through anything like that again."

"Go to your apartment and rest for the balance of the day," the suave doctor ordered her. "I have a double reason for wanting you to do this. You need the rest and I want you to attend our group meeting upstairs tonight."

"If I'm well enough," she said.

"That's understood," he agreed.

She stood up. "You don't think I should consult other medical advice?"

"You have mine," he said. "I suggest you try it before shopping around." And he rose to escort her to the doorway of his office.

The apartment that once had seemed so dominated by the ghost of Walter Glendon had now come to feel like hers. She reached it with a sense of gratitude. Bolting the door behind her she quickly removed her suit and put on a bathrobe before stretching out on the bed to rest. Dr. Martin Gill had been vague in deciding what her medical problem was but at least he didn't seem to think it serious. She hoped he was right.

Now the nagging within her began again. That thin voice mocked her for being such a fool. Reviled her for coming back to place herself in new danger when she could so easily have escaped. It kept clamoring for wisdom on her part before it was too late.

She closed her eyes and refused to listen to it. She was safely back in the old mansion again and that was really all that mattered. Yet she kept wondering where she had gone in her blackout. She had a nervous fear that she might have done something outside the law while she was in that dazed state. It was a shocking thing to not be able to account for hours of your life.

Dr. Martin Gill had mentioned a meeting that evening and said he would like her to attend. She didn't want to. She'd kept away from upstairs and the weird old Madame Helene since the afternoon of the film screening. The doctor had invited her up there many other times. But she'd always avoided the screenings and the close proximity with the strange old woman

139

they demanded. One afternoon in that odd twilight world of a bygone era had been enough.

But she wouldn't be able to as easily avoid the meeting scheduled for tonight. Not after being missing from the office nearly all day. So she must rest for the ordeal and hope it would not turn out to be too trying. She had always wondered about Madame Helene's ability to function with any impressiveness before an audience. Now she'd see for herself. She would also be introduced into another phase of the organization. Evidently Dr. Gill still had confidence in her.

Once again he asked her to look after the front door from seven-thirty until eight. After that she was to go upstairs and join the meeting. She was still feeling strangely confused following her blackout of the morning but well enough to take part in the group meeting. The clients of Madame Helene began arriving promptly at seven-thirty and she directed them to the elevator.

Some of the faces were familiar to her from that other evening when she'd received for the gathering. But there were new ones and she noticed that it was a strangely-mixed group. She kept watching for the hippie who'd been involved in the riot in the Public Gardens but there was no sign of him. However, she still clung to the belief that he had been there before in spite of Dr. Martin Gill's denials.

By five minutes to eight she decided that most of those attending had arrived. This was confirmed when Dr. Martin Gill, immaculately dressed in a dark suit with a hint of a plaid pattern, came to check with her.

"You can come upstairs almost any time now," he said. "I'm beginning our meeting."

"I'll wait until eight or a few minutes after to be sure there are no stragglers," she said.

He was studying her. "You're feeling better?"

"Some," she said. "My head is still light."

He nodded. "I'll give you a check-up in the morning. And I'll look for you upstairs shortly."

She waited by the door as he vanished down the shadowed hall to the elevator. Again she was strongly aware of the confusion she felt. And she wondered why she wasn't able to rationalize and make decisions as she should. Her illness had left her almost an automaton ready to do the suave doctor's bidding. And she wouldn't mind if only that troublesome inner voice didn't angrily complain at odd moments.

An elderly, well-dressed man and woman came and seemed to know their way around the old mansion so she assumed they had been at the meetings before. It was now almost five minutes after eight and she felt it was time to desert her post and make her appearance in the big assembly room of Madame Helene's apartment. She was standing bleakly in the almost dark hall when the doorbell was rung so fiercely that it made her start.

Going to the door she opened it to see a dejected, middle-aged man waiting to come in. He wore a cheap, brown suit that seemed too big for him, his shirt was white with a rumpled collar and his dark tie was knotted loosely. He had an ill-proportioned face, with deep-set shifty eyes and a protruding jaw. His hair was thin and plastered across a balding head.

He came in with a nervous stride and asked her, "Where is Dr. Gill?"

"Upstairs. I think the meeting has already started."

The man scowled. "I wanted to see him personally."

"Are you a regular at the meetings?"

The man nodded. "I've been coming here for a couple of years."

"Then he'll know you."

"He knows me all right," the man said in an ominous way. He gazed down the hall in the direction of the elevator as if undecided whether to attend the meeting or not.

"Perhaps he'll see you after the meeting," she suggested.

The man stood there uneasily. "I need to talk to him."

"That would be the best plan," she said. "I'm going upstairs now. Do you want to take the elevator with me?"

"Are you one of Madame Helene's clients?" the man asked suspiciously.

Diana smiled. "No. I'm the editor of the magazine."

He stared at her strangely. "You took that young man's place."

"Yes. Did you know him?"

"I saw him here. And I know he was killed in a car accident."

"Yes," she said in a small voice. "A tragic business." And a mental picture of the dead Walter Glendon flashed across her mind. His spectral form hadn't come to her with such persistence in the midnight hours lately. Her dreams had taken other, even more eerie shapes.

"His star was in eclipse," the ugly man in the ill-fitting suit said in a kind of slurred voice. "We all die when the stars decree."

"I suppose that's one way of saying it," she agreed, wishing he'd make up his mind whether he wanted to attend the meeting or not instead of just standing there.

He glared at her. "It's the only way. I'm a Taurus and I know my horoscope down to the smallest detail. My wife left me because I live my life by the stars. Took the kids and left me. But I didn't care. I have no choice. I believe we are ruled by the stars. I was born in the first decan of the sign and my death is already ordained at a certain moment."

Diana listened to his harangue with growing alarm. The man was obviously a fanatic. His wild, glaring eyes and offensive manner upset her. Even in her dulled state she knew that he must be bordering on the brink of a nervous breakdown. Probably that was why he wanted to consult Dr. Martin Gill. To seek help. But would the suave doctor offer him aid or play on his weakness!

She said, "I must go upstairs. Have you decided to attend the meeting?"

He smiled at her in a crafty fashion. "I think I will. I'm not liable to come again."

Diana walked with him down the dark hall, nervous in his company. She tried to maintain some sort of casual conversation, saying, "Have you been interested in astrology long?"

"All my life," the man in the ill-fitting suit said. "Wynn was the greatest of them all. He predicted the 1929 depression and the Bank Holiday that followed it."

"He was before my time," she said. "Probably he and Madame Helene were contemporaries."

"She was just beginning in those days," the man said. "But she's the biggest name of them all now."

"So I understand," Diana agreed as they stepped into the elevator.

He stood grimly in a corner of the cage as she set it in creaking motion. "You have a lot to learn about astrology," was his comment.

"I suppose so," she said. And at the same time she was aware of a familiar aroma seeping in the elevator as it moved tortuously towards the upper floor. That smell of spice and roses. It had a particular memory for her. She told the man, "I think they must be using incense of some kind."

He stared at her. "Didn't you know that? They use it every meeting."

"I see," she said.

"Get's everyone in the proper frame of mind," he assured her.

As the elevator came to a halt and she opened the door the smell was more pungent. They walked down the short hall and into the room that served as a meeting place. A number of chairs had been set out for the visitors and Dr. Martin Gill stood before the group on the small stage. Beside him on the chaise lounge sat Madame Helene in one of her dark, ancient gowns

144

with her black hair upswept and garnished by a purple feather of some kind.

The old woman with her mask-like white face restored by plastic surgery sat very still and staring straight ahead of her. In the urns at either side of the stage incense burned, its smoke rising to make fancy bluish patterns in the air. As soon as they entered the big room with its dim lighting the man in the shabby suit moved directly down front to take a seat facing the stage. Diana didn't want to be that near so she took an empty chair by a pretty blonde girl who turned to smile at her.

Dr. Martin Gill was talking in a kind of monotone quite unlike his usual voice. And it struck her he was using a kind of vocal hypnotism to hold the crowd. And he was aided in this by the spice and rose incense whose spiral smoke clouds were filling the big room. For no reason she could understand it all began to seem especially familiar to her. And glancing around she was sure she'd seen some of the faces before. They looked like the monstrous people of her nightmares only their faces were not so distorted.

She coughed as the incense fumes became stronger and she noticed that others occasionally coughed as well. Her head became light and she had a great deal of difficulty following what the suave doctor in his perfectly tailored suit was saying to the devotees of Madame Helene. She had an idea his words were important but they escaped her.

A glance told her that none of the others were paying much attention to the man on the stage. Most of them wore blank, drugged expressions and sat strangely still. Dr. Martin Gill made some sort of introduction and then led Madame Helene to the center of the tiny stage.

The old woman stood there dramatically without uttering a word for a moment. Then she began to speak in that high-pitched old woman's voice. She went on about the tables of the houses and the problem of the T-cross. Diana listened not fully understanding since she didn't know the jargon of the astrological cult well enough yet. But she could see that the old woman was holding her audience.

Or rather that the audience seemed numbed and frozen there. She felt strangely removed from the scene and light-headed. And she wondered if the others had that same sensation. With this in mind she eyed the girl seated next to her. The pretty blonde was watching Madame Helene with an intentness close to worship. But her eyes had a strange glazed look.

Then Madame Helene stopped speaking and Dr. Martin Gill came forward to lead the audience in applause and help the old woman to her seat on the chaise lounge. He returned to address the group briefly and close the session. In the last half-hour of the meeting Diana had noticed that the incense had gone out. Now the room was almost clear of the pungent smoke and smell.

As the meeting came to an end the huge Anna appeared on stage and assisted Madame Helene in making her exit through a rear door. Dr. Martin Gill came down to mingle with those who'd attended the session and almost at once the strange character who had arrived late buttonholed him. Diana watched with keen interest as the man in the ill-fitting suit harangued the smartly-tailored doctor. There was an intensity about the man's manner that clearly marked him as a probable psychotic.

Diana was still standing there studying the two when the pretty blonde girl she'd been seated near, said, "Is this your first time here?"

"I work here," Diana said. "I'm the editor of the magazine."

"Really?" the girl looked at her with new respect. "I think that would be a wonderful job. So interesting!"

"It is," she said quietly. And because she had a theory about the incense, she asked, "Did the incense bother you?"

The blonde girl smiled. "It always does at first. I have a sensitive throat. But later you don't seem to notice it. I'm sure it has a tranquillizing effect. That is why Madame Helene uses it."

This coincided exactly with what she was thinking. "I believe you're right," she said. "It sort of numbed me. I listened to what was said on the stage but I can't remember any of it clearly."

"My head sometimes aches later," the blonde girl said. "But I don't mind. It's a kind of trip, isn't it? And the speaker's words are bound to be engraved on your subconscious. That's what Dr. Gill told me he intended. I asked him about it a few meetings ago."

"So the incense is really a drug he's using deliberately," Diana said in wonder.

"You could say that," the blonde agreed. "I think this is the most exciting thing going on in Boston. Dr.

Gill says I have a marvelous horoscope. And he's offered to let me assist him in some hypnotic experiments."

For no reason she was certain of a chill stab of fear went through her for the pleasant young woman with the chic blonde hair. She said, "Are you sure you want to be involved with hypnotism?"

"I think I'll get a real thrill from it," the girl said her large blue eyes glowing with excitement.

"You're not afraid?"

"Why should I be," the girl said. "I know Dr. Gill is a medical man and an accomplished hypnotist. He used to put some of the big Hollywood stars in a trance. And he says he carried out minor surgery with no other anesthesia other than hypnotism."

"He told you all this?"

The girl nodded brightly. "We're very good friends. He's taken a lot of interest in me."

"I'd think about submitting to hypnotism a bit longer before agreeing to it," was Diana's warning to the girl.

"I like to take chances," the blonde said. "And I know Dr. Gill is a wonderful man. I have perfect trust in him. He is the brain of the Madame Helene organization. Anyone can see that. The old woman is not really competent to carry on much longer."

"She does make the predictions," Diana reminded the girl.

The blonde frowned slightly. "I don't doubt that. There is something other-worldish about her. She probably has second sight. But you can tell her physical health is failing."

"Dr. Gill still depends on her for her prophecies," Diana pointed out.

"I'd expect you to be loyal to her," the blonde girl said with an amused glance. "After all you are employed by her. I hope we meet again." And she walked away to talk to another girl of her own age who was there.

Diana regretted that she couldn't speak out and warn the girl against the move she was making. But warn her about what? That she had a strange feeling about it. The girl wouldn't appreciate that kind of a statement or pay any attention to it.

Dr. Martin Gill had finally gotten away from the ugly man in the shabby suit. He came striding towards Diana with an annoyed expression on his thin face. "This has not been one of the good nights," he observed bitterly. "Let us lead the way out of here. Madame doesn't want to be bothered by this crowd lingering in her apartment."

She went with him and at the door he turned and raised a hand to catch the crowd's attention. "I'm afraid I must ask you all to leave now," he said. "Madame retires early."

The audience filed out past them. And again Diana had the odd feeling that their faces were more familiar than they should be. But her memory of them was a kind of muddled dream. When the last of them had gone to the elevator the suave doctor gave her a look of relief.

"At last that's over," he said.

She gave him an appraising glance. "You sound as if it were an ordeal."

149

"I've handled people for years," he said. "But I must admit the effort always wearies me. I put a great deal of myself in whatever I do."

Diana said, "I found the meeting a strange experience. That incense put me in a kind of fog. I was glad when it cleared." She was testing him to find out how much about its effects as a drug he'd reveal to her. He'd been startlingly frank with the blonde girl but then she was the innocent type who'd never have suspicions anyway.

His shrewd eyes met hers. "It is a rather heady substance," he agreed. "I find it induces the right mood in our clients."

"It surely makes them malleable."

"Astrology is not easy for everyone to understand," the doctor said. "Something like the incense helps open their minds."

She was astounded at the casual way he discussed the mass drugging of his audience. She said, "How can you tell the right amount to burn?"

He looked grimly amused. "I've had a good deal of experience," he said.

They began slowly walking to the elevator. "The aroma of it lingers on," she said. "It's very special. An odor of spice and roses. I remember noticing it before."

"It's harmless," he said as he waited for her to enter the elevator first. As they started down, he said, "You're looking much better than when you came back at noon."

"I was very frightened then," she said. "I still am

when I think about my blackout. I wonder what I did when my mind was a blank."

"Need that worry you? You obviously weren't harmed."

She frowned. "There's more to it than that. I might have harmed someone else without knowing it. I must have wandered for at least two hours after I left here. And I can't remember a single detail of what happened."

The elevator came to a creaking halt. He opened the gate for her. "You need more rest," he said. "Don't worry about getting downstairs at nine in the morning. Come when you feel like it."

"Thank you," she said.

"You worked extra again tonight," he reminded her.

As she left the elevator she hesitated to look back at him in the cage. "I talked with a blonde girl at the meeting tonight," she said. "A very pretty girl. And she told me she was going to assist you in some hypnotic experiments."

The hawk-faced man raised his eyebrows. "You must be mistaken."

"No, she did say it."

His smile was cold. "Then she was making it up. Some of these people tell fabulous lies to make themselves important."

"I had no idea," she said. She was going to mention the ugly man who'd bothered her so much and who she'd seen him in conversation with later. But she didn't. Instead she said goodnight and went on to her apartment.

She listlessly prepared for bed in the same state of apathy that dragged her down constantly these days. She was sure Dr. Martin Gill had been lying when he denied planning a series of hypnotic experiments with the blonde girl. And she was bothered by the aroma of roses and spice which kept on tormenting her after the actual odor had vanished. It was connected with something in her subconscious. She wished she knew what.

That night for the first time in nearly a week the wan ghost of Walter Glendon came back to take his spectral stand at the foot of her bed. He stood there sad-eyed and saying nothing.

CHAPTER NINE

The next morning she woke with the usual miserable aching head. And the memory of that incense in the upper room was so vivid in her mind she could almost smell it in the air of her own apartment. She sat up in bed frowning at the memory of the twenty or so people at the meeting gradually slipping into a dazed state so they were not able to be critical of the faltering Madame Helene.

It was a diabolical scheme on Dr. Martin Gill's part and made it easy for him to sway the converts to his particular brand of astrology. She saw him in a sinister light more clearly than she had for a long time. And she began to worry about her part in all this. And regret that she had broken off contact with Adam Purcell.

If ever she needed the level-headed advice of the young man who'd wanted to marry her, it was now. But she hardly knew how to approach him after the quarrel they'd had on the phone. Wearily dragging herself out of bed she took a shower and dressed. It was another fine September day. And she made a decision. She would type Adam a short note on the office machine and go out at noon and mail it to him.

This plan of action reminded her of her blackout the day before. And of course this worried her. But she was beginning to have other ideas about that strange lapse on her part. Could the wily Dr. Martin Gill have had anything to do with it? He was so adept in the use of drugs and hypnosis that she wouldn't put it past him.

The sullen Anna served her breakfast in silence. As soon as she'd finished her coffee Diana went straight to her own office. The first thing she did was compose the letter to Adam. She strained to think clearly so that she might express herself as she wished. She began by apologizing and ended with the wish he'd get in touch with her as soon as he could. Then she signed the letter and sealed it in an envelope with his New York address.

She'd barely completed the letter and began correcting the proofs of the next issue of the magazine which had come in from the printer when Dr. Martin Gill strolled into her office. The tall, thin man had a pleased air about him and this at once put her on her guard. She moved a large envelope to cover the letter she had waiting to mail to Adam. It seemed important that he shouldn't see it.

The doctor had a copy of the morning paper folded under his arm. He said, "We've gotten ourselves in the news again today. And in a way that can't hurt us."

"Oh?"

He took the paper from under his arm and studied the folded section of it. "For a couple of months Madame Helene has been mentioning Hal Evarts, the labor union executive, and warning him that the stars

154

were unfavorable to him. That this year could be filled with danger for him."

Diana nodded. "I think I've noticed items to that effect in various columns of hers. I wondered about it."

Dr. Martin Gill smiled at her. "Well, you need wonder no longer. It seems that yesterday someone hurled a home-made bomb of some kind in over the open transom of the door of the head office of the union on Washington Street. Evarts and a girl secretary were badly hurt in a blast that rocked the building."

"That's dreadful!" she said. "There's been so much violence lately."

He looked pleased. "I can't worry about the public morals," he said. "I can only congratulate Madame Helene on reading Evarts' horoscope so well. If he'd taken her advice and been more cautious this wouldn't have happened."

"How can you be so sure of that?" she asked. "Couldn't it have been another of those coincidences?"

He put the paper under his arm with a mocking smile for her. "I'd say what you call coincidences have been taking place pretty regularly."

She knew he was right. With puzzled eyes fixed on him, she asked, "What do you make of them?"

"What I always have. My faith in Madame Helene is almost a holy thing. I believe she has second sight and other supernatural powers."

"To me she seems like a stupid and ailing old woman," she said earnestly.

"You underestimate the Madame," he said. "And you will discover she is not so naive as you imagine.

155

I'm disappointed in you that you have so little belief in her."

"I realize I may be wrong," she said. But that inner voice of hers was active again. And today it was louder and more clamoring than ever. It demanded that she speak frankly. That she should not encourage this power-mad man. Stand up for what she believed to be right. As it was now she was going along with him in everything.

"Try to be a little more cooperative," he begged her, his cold gray hypnotist's eyes boring into her. "Madame was pleased to see you at the meeting last night. She told me so. And I was gratified. You know how much I admire you, that I see you in an important post in the future of our organization."

She looked down at her typewriter. "Don't count on it," she said. "My month is nearly up. I may take advantage of your offer that I can leave any time after that if I don't want the job permanently."

"It was a foolish offer," he said. "Until today you've gone along with us very nicely. Don't try to back out now."

"You said it would be all right."

"Because I couldn't imagine the situation coming up. I say you stand to lose a great deal if you leave us."

She gave him a sober look. "I'm not sure I'm suited for your kind of work."

"Nonsense. We picked you because you were born under the right star and at the right moment," he said it with mocking humor.

156

"I'm agnostic enough where astrology is concerned to wonder if that is important," she confessed.

He smiled wryly. "I should take offense at that. But I won't. You see I admire your honesty."

For no reason she could think of, she suddenly asked him, "About that accident. The bomb being thrown into the office of the union leader. When did it happen?"

He gave her a knowing glance. "Yesterday morning."

"What time?"

He shrugged. "I'm not sure. I guess the paper said sometime just before the noon hour." There was a meaningful moment of silence between them. Then he said, "What made you ask?"

"I don't know," she said. She wasn't able to come out with the awful possibility that had just entered her mind. She could only keep it to herself and be tormented by it. Could she, in her spell of blank madness, have been used as the instrument of this evil group? Had they somehow made her visit the office in Washington Street and hurl the bomb?

"What's bothering you?" The doctor's voice sounded as if it were a long distance away.

She braced herself to stifle the upsetting thoughts. And she said, "I was thinking it's a wonder I didn't hear something about it. I was on Tremont Street yesterday. And that can't be too far from where that office is located."

"I'd judge about two long blocks away," he said smoothly. "But it's a busy section and that was a peak

157

time of day. I doubt if there'd be anything to give an indication of what was going on beyond the possible screaming of a siren on the other street. And you'd never notice it with the general noise of traffic and you that far away."

"I suppose not," she said, her lips dry from the fear the possibility of her being involved had brought.

He gave her a significant look. "And anyway you were ill. You had that blank spell."

"Yes."

"Emerging from a blackout you wouldn't be liable to notice much of anything. You were lucky to get back here safely."

"I suppose so."

"So just don't think about it," he advised. "And we can be grateful since such an unfortunate thing had to happen we are going to benefit some from it. All the morning papers have made some brief mention of the Madame's prophecy that he was in grave personal danger."

And with that he went back to his own office leaving her in a desperately troubled state. She went to work but found it almost impossible to concentrate. She tried to recall some of what had happened the previous morning but she couldn't. The worst part of it was that it would be almost impossible to prove she'd been a victim and not a criminal if it should turn she'd been manipulated into throwing the bomb.

No one would believe her fantastic story that she'd either been drugged or hypnotized. They would condemn her for remaining in the grim old mansion and claim she knew exactly what she was doing. If Dr.

Martin Gill had craftily managed to use her in this crime he had achieved a double purpose. He had bound her to the organization by a link of guilt. The small inner voice that had so often tried to warn her was literally thundering out its message now.

But she still attempted to rationalize. Still clung to the hope that she was being too melodramatic about it all. It was normal for Dr. Martin Gill to take advantage of any of the predictions that happened to come true. Any promoter of his type would. It was also likely that a number of predictions had been credited to Madame Helene which hadn't turned out. But these were discreetly forgotten in the organization's publicity releases.

Dr. Martin Gill could dwell all he liked on the supernatural powers possessed by the old woman but she didn't go along with that thinking. She daily felt more certain that the policies of the astrological company were directed solely by the suave doctor. That whatever Madame Helene had been in the past she was nothing more than a front for their activities now.

It was barely possible that Gill was innocent of any wrong-doing. It could be that she had made an error in thinking the hippie who'd started the riot had been the same one she'd seen at the old house several times. And her weird dreams and headaches could be the result of her serious nervous state. The blackout could also be put down to her health. There need be nothing sinister about any of these things.

But as she strained to keep her mind on correcting copy that inner voice berated her for apathy and sloppy thinking. She was deliberately closing her mind

159

to grim facts. Facts such as the change in her own personality since she'd thrown her lot in with the strange group living in the ghostly mansion. If her health was damaged it had been damaged during her stay at the Beacon Street address. The inner voice insisted that something evil was going on there and would continue.

Dr. Martin Gill left for his daily visit to the larger Washington Street headquarters of the astrological publishing corporation. When he'd had time to be well on his way Diana got up from her desk with the letter for Adam and started out to mail it. She paused for a moment at the tiny front office of Miss Carlton.

The gray-haired woman asked, "Going somewhere?"

"I won't be away long," she promised.

"It makes no difference to me," Miss Carlton observed dryly. "I should think you'd need an outing at least once a day. You stay too close to your work."

"I'm sure you're right," she said.

"Of course he doesn't like it," Miss Carlton said, referring to Dr. Martin Gill. "But I notice he goes when and where he pleases."

Diana gave her a bleak smile. "Perhaps he feels the rules don't apply to him."

"He's an arrogant sort," Miss Carlton sniffed. "He gives me little thanks for what I've done. And now that the Madame is getting really decrepit he abuses her."

She frowned. "It's hard to imagine she's old and failing. Her face is still attractive and like a younger woman's."

"Credit that to the face-lifts," the older woman said.

"But look into her eyes and listen to her voice and you know she's very old. Watch the way she walks. She doesn't get far without Anna."

"According to Dr. Gill she has a very weak heart."

"She's had some attacks," Miss Carlton agreed. "I guess they were from her heart. And she'll be worse before she's better."

"That's very likely," Diana agreed. And she quickly got away from the talkative receptionist. It was a pleasant day in the seventy degree range. A typical good fall day.

Just being free of the house gave her a better feeling. She walked to the mailbox on Arlington Street. Then on impulse she crossed the busy street to stroll in the Public Gardens for a little. It was as she reached the other sidewalk that she first knew someone was following her!

Pretending not to know she walked along slowly. She was being followed by a young woman in a dark suit. She had a wan, ordinary face and mousy brown hair.

Diana felt she could stand it no longer and suddenly whirled around to face the young woman. "Who are you?" she demanded. "And why have you been following me?"

The young woman turned scarlet and looked frightened. It was evident she was no professional criminal or anything of that sort. In a trembling voice, she apologized, "I'm sorry. I didn't mean to bother you."

"You have!" Diana said angrily. "What is it you want?"

"To speak to you. I saw you come out of that house on Beacon Street."

She frowned, thinking this must be one of the astrology fanatics. "Well?"

"I hoped you might be able to help me," the girl went on awkwardly. "I guessed you must work in there. And you looked so nice. But I couldn't muster the nerve to come directly up and ask you."

Diana was getting impatient. They were standing away from the middle of the sidewalk and there weren't many people passing. Whatever it was the girl wanted to discuss she wished she would get on with it.

She said, "Please come to the point."

"You don't know me. My name is Ruth Myers. And I guess that doesn't mean anything to you either. Though I have written in to Dr. Gill."

"I'm afraid it doesn't," Diana said.

"I'm Walter Glendon's sister," the girl said with a worried expression on her attractive face. "Did you know him? He lived there and was editor of the magazine."

At once the situation changed for Diana. Her interest was caught. And she saw a faint resemblance to the sad-eyed poet in this younger sister. She said, "I never met your brother. But I do know about him. In fact I have taken his place as editor of Madame Helene's magazine."

The girl showed excitement. "Then maybe you can help me," she said.

"In what way?"

"I've tried to talk to Dr. Gill," the girl said, clutching her handbag nervously, an intense look on her thin

162

face, "but he refuses to see me and when I write him he doesn't answer my letters."

"What are you concerned about?" Diana asked, thinking that the girl was either a mental case or she had something momentous to reveal to her. The weird accident in which Walter Glendon had been at the wheel and both he and Julia James had perished, had always bothered her.

The girl's troubled eyes met hers. "It's about my brother's death."

"Yes?" Diana was determined to reveal no feelings of her own until she'd heard the girl's story. But she was convinced now that what she had to say would be worth listening to.

"I'm not satisfied with the facts they gave out," Ruth Myers said unhappily.

"You think the authorities covered up something?"

"Nothing like that," the girl worried. "I'm thinking more about my brother and his condition before the accident."

"I see," Diana said quietly. She was remembering that sheet of paper with the written message left by Walter Glendon. The oddly morbid message that hinted he might be aware of his coming death. She'd given it to Dr. Gill and he'd kept it. Now she wished she had said nothing about it and hidden it for possible future use. "Please go on," she added.

The slim young girl gave a deep sigh and stared out at the automobile traffic hurtling along Arlington Street as the lights changed. "My husband says I'm getting as neurotic as Walter ever was. He thinks I'm

163

imagining things. But I can't get Walter's death out of my mind."

"It was a tragic accident. I don't blame you for being shocked," she said. At the same time she had an idea the young girl was suggesting something much more sinister than the accident itself.

Ruth Myers turned to her again with despair in her eyes. "Walter wasn't in a fit state of mind to drive that day of the accident. I know it. I talked to him on the phone before he left for New York."

"Why do you insist he wasn't fit to drive?"

"He wasn't like himself at all," she said. "But then he'd gradually been behaving more strangely. That afternoon he was almost incoherent. My phone call seemed to upset him."

"Did he say that?"

"He implied it," Ruth Myers said. "He said he didn't want to talk. That he couldn't bring himself to say goodbye. He was going and he wasn't coming back."

Diana stared at the girl incredulously. "He said that? But I thought he was merely driving Julia James' car to New York and coming back by plane the next morning."

"That's what the papers said," Walter Glendon's sister spoke scornfully. "But his story was different. He talked wildly. Mumbled something about death being welcome when your destiny ruled it."

"Had he ever said such things to you before?"

"Not so plainly," Ruth Myers said. "But he'd been talking in a weird way for weeks. The last time he came to the house, my husband and I have a house in

Brockton, he wasn't himself at all. He'd always had a fanatical belief in astrology but this was different."

"In what way?"

The girl hesitated, seeming unable to explain herself. "I don't know," she said at last. "He acted as if he was under the influence of some drug or was having a nervous breakdown. He paced continually and sometimes mumbled to himself. When he did talk to us he kept raving about the stars being against him. I begged him to see a psychiatrist."

"What was his reaction?"

"I just couldn't seem to reason with him at all," the girl said brokenly. "It was then I called Dr. Gill. I knew my brother needed treatment or help of some kind. I told the doctor who I was and why I was calling. He answered in the most abrupt manner that he saw nothing wrong with Walter and I would be well advised to mind my own business."

"What was your reply to that?"

Ruth Myers shrugged hopelessly. "I didn't know what to say. My husband wasn't too fond of Walter anyway. He thought he was a neurotic type. He said I'd better take the doctor's advice. And I did though I wasn't happy about the way things were with Walter."

Diana was trying to get it all in place. "And you never did see your brother alive again?"

"No."

"But you did talk to him on the phone?"

"Yes. I was very concerned about him. So I phoned every few days. The last time I called was the day he was leaving for New York with that James woman. And he acted as I've told you."

Diana asked, "What about Julia James? Was Walter in love with her?"

"I don't believe it. Though I think she was interested in him. He was a very intelligent person and talented. He wrote wonderful poetry. I had an idea she might have been a bad influence on him. From all I've read about her she was wild and self-willed. I thought she might have started him taking drugs."

"Did he ever mention her to you?"

"Only to say that they were friends. Julia James was interested in astrology and depended on Madame Helene for career advice. She spent a lot of time visiting that house on Beacon Street."

Diana studied the girl and wondered what her story might mean. She was shaken by some of the things this sister of the dead Walter Glendon had told her. And once again she was having dark suspicions that Madame Helene had a way of making her predictions come true. A way that might well include murder!

"What is it you hope to do now?" Diana asked.

The girl's face clouded. "I don't honestly know. Perhaps I'm looking for revenge. I can't help Walter but if that awful Dr. Martin Gill caused his death I'd like to see him pay for it."

Diana stared at her. "How do you think Dr. Gill could have caused your brother's death?"

"By allowing him to drive that James girl to New York when he knew he simply wasn't fit to get behind the wheel of a car."

"But your brother knew how to drive?"

"He drove perfectly when he was well," the girl said. "I don't think he was well that night."

"I see," she said quietly. She was fairly sure the other girl had no idea of the bigger and more horrifying possibility involved in the deaths of her brother and the girl singer. And she didn't propose to hint any of this to her at the moment.

"I thought you might have heard something," the girl said. "You've been living in the house for several weeks. I decided to try and talk to you and see if you'd help me."

"I wish I could," Diana said with a sigh. "But I don't know how. Even if your brother was upset it still could have been a normal accident. He made a miscalculation in his driving and it cost him his life."

The girl's eyes were empty and sad. "I think he was determined to die. That someone at that old house forced the idea on him. I believe my brother committed suicide and took that girl to her death with him. And if so I'd like to do something about it."

Diana frowned. "That's an extravagant theory, Mrs. Myers."

"I know," the girl said in a low voice.

"Still, I'm glad you mentioned this to me," Diana said carefully. "If only because I may be able to find out some facts about what went on at the house and set your mind at rest."

"Thank you," the girl said warmly. "I've told you all this and I don't believe I even know your name."

"I'm Diana Lewis," she said. "And I'm editing the magazine now. Did your brother ever tell you anything about Madame Helene?"

"He had an awe of her. He was sure she dealt in the supernatural. That she had powers beyond the under-

167

standing of most people. He claimed she had a ghostly presence."

Diana's face was grim. "That's not a bad description of her."

"Walter said she was very old. Maybe a hundred. But he said it was Dr. Martin Gill who carried on the actual operations of the company. And that is why I blame Dr. Gill for whatever went wrong with my brother. And also, Dr. Gill behaved in a suspicious manner when he refused to talk to me about the state Walter was in."

"You don't blame the influence of Madame Helene for what happened?"

"No," the other girl said solemnly. "I blame Dr. Gill. In my opinion that singer, Julia James, was taking drugs. And Dr. Gill allowed her to drag Walter into it."

Diana hesitated a moment. "You know that Madame Helene predicted Julia James' death on the exact date that it happened?"

"I've read that. But I don't believe it."

"No?" Diana was mildly startled.

"No. I think she made some dark prediction in a general way and then changed it to suit the occasion. Before Walter changed so he joked to me about the clever way Dr. Gill had latched onto the JFK assassination. I was shocked but he shrugged it off as a justifiable means to get publicity for the charts they sold."

Diana said, "Some of their methods do appear unscupulous to those on the outside."

Ruth Myers said, "I have deep faith in astrology.

168

Though I'm not as fanatical as Walter was. I'm a Capricorn and I married a Taurus and we're very happy. I think that is because our signs are compatible. And I've used astrology to guide me in other ways, in scientific ways. But I'm not sure that is how Madame Helene is conducting her business. I think in order to make money Dr. Gill has branched out into sensationalism."

"You could be right."

"I don't want to hurt anyone," the girl worried. "But I think Walter wasn't given a chance."

"Let me make some inquiries," Diana suggested. "Give me your home address and phone number. If and when I learn anything I'll get in touch with you."

"I'd be very grateful," the girl said. And she took a pad of paper from her handbag and wrote the information down. Then she handed it to her.

They parted and Diana made her way across the street in a kind of fog. The meeting with this sister of Walter Glendon's had opened up a whole new avenue of possibilities. It had helped bring her out of her apathy. She'd emerged a little in the morning but not enough. Now perhaps she would persevere until some of the mystery surrounding that house on Beacon Street had been solved.

Walter Glendon's sister seemed convinced that her brother had gradually succumbed to some strange influence. She blamed it on Julia James and drugs. But was she blaming the right person? Diana strongly doubted it. For wasn't she also experiencing the same kind of personality change? Hadn't she been sinking into a bizarre type of mental fogginess?

And last night she'd witnessed Dr. Martin Gill brazenly bring the entire group at the lecture under the influence of that powerful incense with its pungent rose and spice odor. If he would do that he wouldn't hesitate to use even more vicious drugs on individuals whom he wanted to control. And he was an accomplished hypnotist as well. If Walter Glendon had been sent to his death to bring about a prediction of Madame Helene's there was only one person who could be responsible, Dr. Martin Gill.

Had he also used his evil talents to send her out on an errand of death and destruction yesterday? Would she find herself unable to oppose the horror he could be unleashing because he had manipulated her into a position of guilt?

CHAPTER TEN

On her way back to the four-storied brick mansion on Beacon Street Diana made several decisions. Her first impulse had been not to return to the forbidding house of shadows and evil. But she came to the conclusion she was not yet ready for that. Before she left she must try and find out more of what was really going on behind those thick walls and shuttered windows.

And she also needed to discover how deep in the mire of horror she'd sunk, know the meaning of the blackout she'd had and what lay behind it. If she were to expose the terrifying happenings directed by Dr. Martin Gill, she must learn more about them. And that meant remaining in the house. If she were lucky she'd get a quick reply from her letter to Adam Purcell. There was no question that she needed his help and advice.

In the meantime she would work to discover what she could in the old house. It frightened her that Anna had a key to the apartment she occupied. She'd complained to Dr. Martin Gill about this and he'd put her off in his usual urbane fashion. When she was in the apartment she could bolt the door and feel reasonably safe. But when she was working downstairs or just out, the swarthy woman could probably enter it at will.

She made up her mind to speak to the suave doctor again. Also, she decided that from now on she would prepare all her own meals. She'd been taking some of them downstairs since the offer of her food as an extra had been made to her. But she did not want to have Anna serving her anymore. She had a fear the peasant woman might be putting something in her food or drink. Anna hated her and was capable of almost anything.

Because this meant she needed some groceries she found a friendly shop on a side street and bought a small supply of the most necessary items. Other things she could get later. The proprietor of the tiny neighborhood delicatessen assured her the store was open every night until midnight and sometimes later.

This was good news. It not only offered her an excuse to get away from the grim mansion at night if she felt the need. It also gave her at least one person she could appeal to if she were in trouble. By establishing herself as a customer at the delicatessen she would become identifiable in the mind of the owner. He would feel some small obligation to help her or summon the police if she came to him for assistance.

Satisfied with this first small move she went back to the house. Miss Carlton was busy on the phone when she entered the cool, dark hallway so she hurried by her door so there would be no awkward questions raised about the groceries she was carrying. She took

172

the elevator up to the second floor and installed the groceries in the kitchen of her apartment. Both the range and the refrigerator were working which was helpful.

When she'd finished taking care of the groceries she prepared to go down to her office again. The events of the morning had brought her back to an almost normal resemblance of her old self. Her head was much clearer and she was acting with a purpose for the first time in some weeks. She only hoped she wasn't doing it too late.

The sister of Walter Glendon had touched her with her pathetic story. And she felt one of the first things she should do was try to find out some more about the young man who'd been her predecessor on the magazine. Clues to the rest of the puzzle could well be concealed in the true facts about him.

She went to Miss Carlton's office as her first move. Finding the prim woman not busy for the moment, she asked her, "You've spoken of Walter Glendon occasionally, do you think he changed a lot just before the time of his fatal accident?"

Miss Carlton frowned. "I never did like him. But that last week he was really queer and jumpy. He'd say things that didn't make sense and he wasn't doing his work on the magazine at all. I can't think why Dr. Gill kept him on."

This information fitted in with what Ruth Myers had told her. Diana was anxious to get all the news she could from the gray-haired woman when she was in a talking mood. Often she wouldn't discuss the happenings in the old house at all.

She said, "What was the attraction between him and Julia James?"

"I never could decide that," the older woman admitted. "Julia James was a famous star and that Walter Glendon was a nobody. Yet she seemed to like him. And I guess that was one of the reasons Dr. Gill didn't fire him. The doctor always catered to Julia."

"Julia came to this house a lot?"

"At least twice a week," the prim Miss Carlton said. "She lived her life by the rules set down by Madame Helene."

Diana smiled bleakly. "Isn't it strange she ignored the warning about her death date."

"Oh, she didn't," Miss Carlton said quickly. "I handled a call between her and Dr. Gill when they talked about that awful prediction the Madame made. Julia James was in a frantic state. She was crying over the phone and asking the doctor what she would do."

"You heard all this yourself?"

The older woman crimsoned. "I don't listen in to calls as a rule. But she was so upset I didn't want to miss it. She said she'd decided to pass up an engagement in New York becaue it wouldn't be safe to travel there. Dr. Gill said he wouldn't recommend her using a train or plane under the circumstances. Nor would he advise that she drive her car as she usually did. But he thought she'd be safe enough if she had someone else drive the car. And he suggested Walter Glendon."

"Dr. Gill actually named Walter as a possible driver for her?"

"Yes. I was some surprised because I didn't even

know that Walter could drive. Julia liked the idea and said Walter was a nice young man. And would the doctor ask him to do it. The doctor said he would and that was how it all came about."

"I'd think Walter Glendon was a poor choice to drive in the nervous state everyone seems to agree he was in," Diana said.

"I agree," Miss Carlton said. "But people do strange things. The doctor never seemed to worry about it."

"How did Dr. Gill act when the accident was reported?"

"First he wanted to know for sure how badly hurt the two were. And when he heard they were dead he went straight upstairs and told Madame Helene."

"I suppose he had to take advantage of the publicity the tragedy brought Madame Helene no matter how upset he was."

"I'd say that was about it," Miss Carlton agreed. "And it's always been my opinion that Walter Glendon was as crazy as a coot when he set out to drive that poor girl to New York. She'd have been safer with a drunken man at the wheel."

Calls started coming in again to take Miss Carlton's attention and so the conversation ended. Diana returned to her own office in a sober mood. All that the older woman had said fitted in with what she'd been told. The picture was growing more ominous all the time. She forced herself to do some more copy-editing but her mind kept wandering.

Dr. Martin Gill returned a few minutes before two. He paused for a moment at her office. "I trust you're

175

feeling better," was his greeting as he stood in the doorway.

"Yes, I am," she said. And by way of testing him out she said, "I had a rather strange phone call from a young woman named Ruth Myers. She claimed she was the sister of Walter Glendon and wanted to see me. I told her I hadn't met her brother and couldn't be of any help to her."

The doctor nodded approvingly. "That's exactly the line to take. Otherwise we'd both be tormented by that unfortunate girl. From what Walter said to me I gather there's something a little off in her head. She's given to wild imaginings."

"I understand that Walter Glendon was hardly normal the last few weeks of his life," she said, probing for information. "A thread of insanity must run in the family."

The suave doctor smiled in his casual way. "I'd say that he was overwrought. I wouldn't call him mentally unbalanced. He was a sensitive youth and very much in love with Julia James. She didn't take their romance as seriously as he did."

"Oh?" she raised her eyebrows.

"They had a quarrel but made it up. He was very worried that their reconciliation wouldn't last. And that is why I believe he wanted to act as her chauffeur on the trip to New York. He begged me to let him go on the grounds that it wouldn't be safe for Julia to drive with Madame Helene's dread prediction hanging over her head."

Diana listened to this with growing awareness of the crafty evil of the doctor. He was deliberately twisting

176

the story. Everything he said was in reverse to the truth.

"So you allowed him to drive her?" she said, pretending to believe all he said.

"Yes. I see now that it was wrong of me, especially with him in his high-strung state. Julia loved to tease him. I suspect she started it along the way and in a rage he deliberately ran them into that truck."

This was an interesting new account. Of course it wasn't true. But at least Dr. Martin Gill was admitting that it was a personality defect on Walter Glendon's part that had brought about the accident. This was revealing since she believed the evil doctor had deliberately set things up for the accident to happen.

She said, "I suppose you were beseiged by reporters."

"We had the usual problems with the press."

"But you must expect that with Madame Helene making such predictions," Diana said. And by way of diverting him from the fact she was deliberately dredging up some of these past things, she added, "I believe the predictions would make a good feature article for some future issue of the magazine."

He looked pleased. "A fine idea. Why don't you write it?"

"I don't know whether I have enough background in astrology."

"My library is lined with astrological books," he said. "Every kind of reference work you can think of. They are all open to you. I want to see you advance yourself in the field. It is necessary for my plan to feature you in the organization."

"I'll think about it," she said. And rising from her desk, she told him, "There is one other thing."

"Yes?"

"If I'm to remain on here I must have more independence. I know Anna has a key to my apartment. And I don't feel safe while she has it. I spoke to you about this before."

"I believe you did," he admitted. He frowned. "Be patient a few days longer. You know how Madame Helene caters to Anna. I have to be careful not to cross her."

She knew this was just a ruse to stall for time. He had no intention of getting her the key. But she made no argument about it, though she did say, "I've also decided I'll take my meals in the apartment in future, also because Anna bothers me. And I think I'll enjoy the novelty of doing my own cooking."

"Why do the extra work?" he asked with a puzzled look.

"I think it will be good for me."

The doctor looked bleak. "Whatever you like," he said. "The main thing is I need you here. You are free to do as you like if you'll stay."

She knew his apparent reasonableness was as much a fraud as everything else about him. And she was beginning to wonder about those past days in Hollywood. What sort of doctor had he been? And how had he won the friendship of all those dead stars whose photos were on his wall? Perhaps he hadn't known them at all. The signatures on the portraits could have been forged by him. It could be a crafty trick to give him stature.

After he left her she worked for awhile. But her head began its familiar aching and the letters of the copy danced before her eyes. She was thankful when five o'clock came and she could retreat to her own apartment. Dr. Martin Gill had already gone up for the afternoon screening of an old movie for Madame Helene. As Diana went up to her own floor in the groaning elevator she could picture that fantastic scene in the upper apartment.

Old Madame Helene would be seated on the chaise lounge following every scene in the movie with avid interest. Seated there in the darkness it would all come alive for her again, the ghostly images of the people who had been her friends and co-workers would be there for her to watch. And likely she herself would be up there with those spectral shadows. The ancient astrologer was lost in that past; the wily Dr. Martin Gill was taking advantage of her madness to use her as a cover-up for his vicious racket. There was no doubt he'd turned what had likely been a respectable astrological publishing house into something shady.

Some of the old apathy came over her as she went about preparing her evening meal. She wasn't hungry but knew she should eat. While she was working in the kitchen she turned on her small FM battery radio. It was news time and one of the first items to catch her attention and fill her with sheer horror was an account of a subway accident. The announcer spoke in an excited fashion, "Boston has the oldest subway system in North America. And strangely it has had a record of few accidents. This record was marred late this afternoon when a crowded train ran into the rear of an-

179

other in a tunnel beyond Back Bay station. At least six people are dead as a result of the collision and another fifty or more injured. The exact figures of dead and injured cannot be verified until later but this was the last report. The present theory as to the cause of the accident is that the driver of the second train had some kind of fainting spell. Since he is among the dead this will never be known as a fact. At any rate he seems to have made no attempt to prevent the collision. An aura of grim mystery surrounds the tragic accident. This is increased by the fact that a noted Boston astrologer, Madame Helene, has been warning of a possible accident in our bus, elevated or subway system for some months. So another prediction of this incredible woman has come true!"

The reporter moved on to another news item but Diana was no longer listening. She was standing there leaning on the counter for support. She fought off the fainting feeling that had swept over her. Once the shock and resulting nausea had passed she thought she would be all right. But she was filled with horror at this latest bombshell. All she could think of was that the vicious doctor had arranged another accident.

But then the prediction had been vague and covered all the various transportation systems. It was a good bet for a minor or major accident to happen somewhere along the lines of one of these systems during a period. Madame Helene had been playing it safe enough. And then with her incredible luck this had happened and she was in the limelight again. So perhaps it had been a genuine accident.

One thing she knew. And that was that she wanted

180

more information about what had happened. She recalled that the little delicatessen carried newspapers in addition to its regular food line; she made up her mind to go out at once and get a copy of the evening edition of the *Globe*.

She went downstairs and the first person she encountered was Dr. Martin Gill. His eyes were bright. "Have you heard the latest?"

"Yes," she said in a hushed voice.

"What incredible luck the Madame has in her predictions," he exulted. "The Washington Street office just got in touch with me and claim their switchboard is alive with calls. And the reporters are showing up there now that most of the rescue work is over in the tunnel."

"What a dreadful tragedy it is," she said with distaste.

He glanced at her somewhat abashed. "I'm sorry. I didn't mean to let the proprieties be dashed aside. I'm shocked by the accident."

She said, "I have to get a few things at the delicatessen. I'll be back shortly."

"Can't you phone for them?" he asked.

"No. I like to see what I'm ordering," she said.

"Take care," he warned. "Boston streets at night are not as safe as they used to be."

"I'll remember that," she promised. "Does Madame Helene know of the collision?"

"Not yet," he said. "Because of her physical state I want to find exactly the best moment to break it to her. I don't dare risk her having another heart attack. I doubt if she'd survive it."

181

"That's true," she agreed. The phone rang again and he had to leave her to enter his office and take the call. He was still talking to someone in New York when she left. She stepped outside and took a deep breath of the cool evening air. It would soon be dusk. At least she was free of the house for a little. Just being near Dr. Martin Gill frightened her.

She walked swiftly along the pavement her high heels pounding out a crisp tattoo. At Arlington she turned the corner and soon came to the delicatessen. The diminutive elderly owner waddled over to her with a bright gleam in her eyes. "So you've joined the crowd who want the evening paper. The accident brought a real run on them tonight. I've only got a few put under the counter for special customers." He gave her a friendly nod. "You can have some of them."

"That's very good of you," she said, not wanting to miss the chance as she fumbled for a coin to pay him.

He brought out the paper and frowned at the front page filled with photos of the accident. "What an awful thing," he said. "My wife almost was caught in the wreck. She was going to visit a friend but changed her mind at the last minute."

She paid him and took the paper. "How fortunate."

"Yep," he said philosophically. "That's how it is these days. You never know."

"No, you don't," she agreed nervously. She wanted to study the paper but didn't trust herself to do so there in front of him. At that moment another customer came in and took the little proprietor's attention. She was grateful and quickly slipped out of the store.

On the street she opened the paper and saw the large photographs of the wrecked cars. They were on their sides on the track and badly crumpled. It seemed as if more people should have been killed in such a frightful crash. Her eyes wandered from the two large pictures at the top of the page to some smaller ones below.

And her eyes went wide with sheer horror!

She was looking at a face all too familiar to her. The face of the man in the ill-fitting suit who'd arrived late for the meeting the other night. She couldn't mistake the ugly features and the loose jaw. It was the man who'd wanted to talk privately to Dr. Martin Gill and who had plagued the suave medical man after the meeting. She remembered that Gill had come to her in a rage at being bothered by him.

And there he was in the photo which was tagged, "Dead driver of the second train." It was enough. This man had been in exactly the same mental state as Walter Glendon before he'd driven that car into a truck. It was the identical pattern all over again. She put the paper under her arm and began slowly walking back to the house on Beacon Street.

The memory of Dr. Martin Gill's exultant mood when she'd left him only a quarter-hour ago sickened her. He didn't care! He was only interested in the benefits the organization would receive in sales from another prediction come true. Gill must have observed the near-demented subway operator for months. He knew that he was a psychotic and with a little prodding would do some terrible thing. And he had allowed it to happen!

That was the dreadful truth! There had been no need for the suave doctor to put the unstable subway operator up to any diabolical plan. All he had to do was encourage his upset state of mind and do nothing. Sooner or later this was calculated to produce results. And so it had!

Fear shadowed her face as she drew near the somber old brick building. Did she dare go back in? Could she do anything else? She was involved too deeply to try and escape now, not until she had sufficient evidence to prove what she suspected. And what she suspected was at the very least, murder by influence!

Who would be the next expendable victim to enrich Dr. Martin Gill's shady empire? It could be her; already she had been used. She wasn't even sure what she'd been involved in, though she suspected she might have been the one who perpetrated the Washington Street bombing of the union headquarters under hypnotic and drug influence. Surely she'd come to herself on Tremont Street only a short time later. And very close to the scene of the bombing.

She knew she must somehow keep up a pretence of naiveté and not show her true feelings at this time. But it was going to be difficult, perhaps impossible. She could only brace herself for the ordeal and hope. Keep telling herself it was necessary if she had any thought of exposing Dr. Martin Gill's cruel hoax.

She let herself in the front door with a feeling of panic, and quickly made her way down the long dark hallway to the elevator. She had to pass the various offices and as she came near Dr. Martin Gill's she heard his voice on the phone again. It was turning out to be a busy evening for him. It was to be expected. The story of the disaster would get national and even international coverage and mention of the prediction by Madame Helene would undoubtly be in most of the accounts.

She came abreast of the doorway just as he put the phone down. He saw her and motioned to her to come in. She did and received a second shock when she discovered the pretty blonde girl she'd sat next to at the meeting in an easy chair at the other end of the room. The girl nodded to her and smiled.

Dr. Martin Gill's hawk face was as bright with excitement as she'd ever seen it. "The response to the accident story is unbelievable," he told her. "I want you to scrap the lead article in the next issue of the magazine and I'll provide you with an entirely new story dealing with Madame Helene's predictions."

"Very well," she said quietly.

"Jean Dixon better look to her laurels," the doctor said with smiling satisfaction. He glanced at the blonde girl happily and turning to Diana again, added, "I imagine you've met Mary Wright."

"Yes," she said. "At the meeting the other night."

"We sat next to each other," the blonde volunteered. "I'm afraid I've come at a bad time for my hypnotism instructions." This last was directed to the doctor in an apologetic manner. "I can go and come back some other time."

"Not at all," Dr. Martin Gill said. "You've taken your time to come here. I'll somehow manage to give you at least a half-hour. If you don't object to these phone calls interrupting us."

185

"I think it's terrific," Mary Wright said enthusiastically. "Just imagine Madame Helene predicting the accident."

Dr. Martin Gill raised his hand in a modest gesture. "Please remember, my dear, she didn't predict this particular disaster. She merely insisted there was going to be a serious accident in one of the suburban travel mediums. That is rather different."

"It's close enough to impress me," the girl said.

The suave doctor smiled. "I don't think anyone questions the psychic talents of Madame."

Diana was so enraged at his complacency she couldn't resist holding up the paper for him to see the photo of the train operator. "Do you recognize him?" she asked.

Dr. Martin Gill gave her an apprehensive glance that told her he already had seen the paper, knew all about it in any case. He gave the photo a casual study. "Yes," he said. "I believe he has attended some of our meetings. An odd chap."

"Very odd indeed," she said dryly. "He insisted on talking to you the other night."

The hawk-faced doctor met her glance with an assured one of his own. She needed to give him credit for brazen coolness. "I remember. He was a bore. Almost incoherent. It could be that it was his attending the meetings that gave the Madame the basis for her prediction."

Diana frowned. "In what way?"

He spread his hands. "Very simple. The shadow of approaching disaster must have been over him for weeks. Madame Helene would be aware of it through her psychic sensitivity. Though she mightn't be sure who the doomed person was or what the warning meant exactly."

She folded the paper under her arm again. "That's a very interesting explanation," she said. "Are you going to mention it to the press?"

He shook his head. "No. I think these things are more effective with the public if we attempt no explanation. I'd say the fact he occasionally came here is of relatively minor importance."

Very clever of you, was her thought. But she said, "Perhaps, that's true." She gave Mary Wright a parting nod. "Good luck with your lesson."

"Thank you," the girl said in her friendly fashion.

Dr. Martin Gill followed Diana to the door. "Don't forget what I said about removing that article from the copy."

"I won't," she promised.

As soon as she stepped into the ancient elevator and moved the switch she closed her eyes. The elevator creaked upward. The short discussion with the suave Gill had been an enlightening one. She knew now how he was going to handle the situation. And she was at once fearful for the pleasant Mary Wright. There could be no question that he was grooming the pretty blonde girl for some purpose.

She left the elevator at the second floor and went to her room. After she'd bolted the door she sat down and read the entire account of the accident. Then she studied the ugly features of the dead train operator. It was like one of her nightmares. Only this was one from which there would be no awakening.

187

Somewhere up on the top floor the ailing and elderly Madame Helene would be sitting lost in her dream world of a Hollywood yesterday. Perhaps the silent and diabolical Anna would be hovering near, sullenly watching the old woman. Diana had never been sure whether Anna's loyalty was to Madame Helene or whether she was really a puppet of Dr. Martin Gill's. In this weird house it was hard to be certain.

One thing she did know. Everyone, and this included her, who entered the grim four-storied house was somehow twisted and influenced by the evil that lurked there. She did not understand how she had succumbed to malign influence but she had. Her intellect had been numbed and her physical state corrupted to the extent that she had quietly gone along with the doings of the Madame Helene organization.

At least now she'd recovered to the extent that she knew what was going on and ready to oppose the depraved wickedness of the forbidding Dr. Gill. But she must realize that he would make a wily adversary. This gave her the uneasy feeling that he was not yet finished with her.

CHAPTER ELEVEN

She had not thought sleep would come easily. But it was far worse than that. In her badly upset state sleep would not come at all. She had left a small lamp turned on. When sleep still eluded her, it was natural to blame the lamp. So she switched it off to leave the room dark; it did no good. She moved restlessly in the bed, with each position giving away to uneasiness and making her take another one.

The reality of the disaster tormented her mind. And she re-lived those moments when she'd talked with the near-mad operator of the wrecked train. He had gone on in a morbid vein showing an antagonistic attitude to everyone and everything. He'd spoken of his dedication to astrology and that it had cost him his marriage. His mental state must have been exactly like that of the doomed Walter Glendon.

She sat up in bed and turned the lamp on again. A glance at her wristwatch told her it was past two and she hadn't slept yet. She had a wild impulse to put a phone call through to Ruth Myers, the sister of Walter Glendon. She wanted to discuss the accident with the girl and point out the similarities with what had happened to her brother. But she curbed herself from the impetuous gesture. There was a chance the hawk-faced Dr. Martin Gill might still be up and around. And he could easily intercept and hear any call made by her on the house line.

She stared across the murkily-lighted room as she considered the impeccably dressed Gill with his cruel face and domed bald head. He was the evil genius of all that was happening. As far as she was concerned both Madame Helene and Anna were only tools in his hands. And again she wondered whether he actually possessed a medical degree as he claimed, and just what his position had been in Hollywood.

It was while she was deliberating on this that she first became aware of the odor of roses and spice filtering into her room. At once she recognized it as the incense which the insidious Dr. Gill used for his group meetings, the incense with the properties of a tranquilizing drug. And each moment the smell of it became stronger. She could actually see wispy blue curlings of the stuff in the air of her room. It was surging in! A touch of light-headedness warned her that she was beginning to react to it.

Quickly she snatched up a hankie and held it over her nostrils. At the same time she tried to guard against breathing too deeply. The incense was literally pouring into her room. She was out of bed and staring up at the ceiling with frightened eyes now. She could see where the incense fumes were coming from—through the air-conditioning vent!

No doubt it was another of the evil doctor's schemes. He had somehow fixed the air vent so he could drive these noxious, drugged fumes down to her. As the room became blue with the incense she ran across to the tiny kitchen and closed the door. Then she opened the single window and took a gasping breath of the fresh night air.

As she did so her mind was moving at a hectic rate. And she realized why she'd experienced her personality change. Every night while she was asleep Dr. Martin Gill had thus systematically drugged her. Under the influence of the rose and spice incense she had experienced those weird dreams. But she hadn't awakened as the drug also was a powerful sedative. By the time she awoke at the normal time in the morning the odor of roses and spice had evaporated.

But her system still suffered from the harmful effects of the drug. And it was her subconscious that had recognized it when the doctor had used it in small concentration at the meeting. But he'd been administering her massive doses of it nightly in her bedroom. She remained in the kitchen trembling in the knowedge of her danger.

After a little she cautiously opened the door and saw that the concentration of smoke in the bedroom was lessening. In fact there was only a hint of the give-away smell left. By morning it would have completely evaporated. That was how she'd come to have the headaches for which there was no apparent reason. The evidence had vanished in the night. Now, with the aid of the open window in the kitchen the room soon was aired again.

She stood studying the vent. How clever of the doctor! And no wonder he felt he could smugly count on her cooperation in the future. He was gradually changing her into a brain-washed zombie with this drugged incense. The night before the morning of her blackout he'd undoubtedly given her a doubly-strong dose. And when she'd gone downstairs how simple for him to call her into his office, give her the package containing the bomb, and have her deliver it under hypnotism.

The big question now was how to protect herself. She needed all her wits about her if she was to leave this house alive and gain the proof of guilt she needed against Dr. Martin Gill. The vent of the air-conditioner was the weapon he was using against her. She must somehow find a way to at least lessen its danger. For if she remained in the house she would certainly sleep during the hours when the fumes would be sent to weaken her.

She went out to the kitchen and found a screwdriver and hammer under the stainless steel sink. Still with no idea of what she might do she came back into the room. Next she cleared off a sturdy table and placed it directly under the air vent. Using a chair she got up on the table and checked the screws holding the aluminum vent in place. The screws had medium-size heads and her screwdriver was large. But she raised her arms, stood almost on tip-toe and with great effort was able to begin removing the screws. One gave her a lot of trouble, seeming to be stripped. But at last she was able to take off the grilled cover of the vent.

Staring up into the darkness of the piping she saw a gaping black void that narrowed to a size about three inches in diameter. It seemed to her if she could find something to at least partly block off the piping she would have a measure of protection. Glancing about the room she spied a small black-velvet covered pillow on one of the easy chairs. It looked to her like the ideal size for her purpose. She stepped down from the table and got the pillow. It was filled with feathers or some other soft material and could be molded into the required space.

Back on the table she stuffed the pillow in the ceiling opening so that it was tightly against the air-conditioning pipe. Then she carefully replaced the vent and screwed it in place. From now on she'd have no air-conditioning, she thought grimly, but she wouldn't find herself being systematically drugged either.

She moved the table back and cleaned the plaster particles from the rug to hide what she'd done. She was convinced that both Anna and the doctor went through her room every so often. It was ironic that air-conditioning had persuaded her to accept the job. And the same air-conditioning had been the weapon used against her. The room was so cleared of the incense now she had no hesitation in closing the kitchen window.

With a feeling of something accomplished she got back in bed and turned out the light. Weary from her effort and lack of sleep, relaxed in the knowledge she had struck back against her enemy, she closed her eyes. And the sleep she'd sought for so long without success came quickly and naturally.

Next morning reporters came to the house on Beacon Street for the first time since Diana had been working there. Miss Carlton complained about the extra bother they created. But they were shown into Dr. Martin Gill's office, a half-dozen of them, and he gave them a short interview. Diana stood in the background taking it all in.

The suave doctor was politely smug, but he fended off all tricky questions. Yes, Madame Helene was possessed of psychic ability and had predicted the accident. No, she was not well enough to greet the press. She was a very old woman and ill; her health must be protected. What role did he play in the organization? He was physician and advisor to the aged astrologer. Did he believe in astrology? Yes. He had long been a disciple of the science of the stars. Had he practiced in Hollywood and were all the stars whose photos were on the wall known to him? He had lived in Hollywood years ago and many of the dead stars had been his close friends, but he had not practiced actively all those years. Did he think Madame Helene would continue to make valid predictions? He could not promise. But her prophecies were based on her study of the stars and her communion with the supernatural. With this in mind it was reasonable to assume she would continue to predict events.

Diana received the impression that the reporters were not wholly taken in by the suave Dr. Gill. But he was a story and they didn't mind building it up for their own benefit. He dismissed them after a short period and Miss Carlton escorted them to the door.

When the doctor and Diana were alone, he said, "I think I handled that as well as I could. We're in a touchy spot at the moment. Any mistakes in public relations could do us serious harm."

She gave him a meaningful look. "I think they would have liked to talk directly with Madame Helene."

"Of course," he said with contempt. "They would also like to talk to the President or the Governor. But these people give interviews when it suits them. It is not a suitable time for the Madame to appear."

"Does she know about the subway collision yet?"

"No," he said shortly. "I may decide not to tell her."

She went back to her own office and worked on the next issue. She'd only been at her desk for a half-hour when her phone rang. It was a long distance call from New York. In a moment Adam Purcell was on the line.

"I received your letter last night late when I came back to my apartment," he said. "I needn't tell you it was welcome."

Her relief at hearing his pleasant, youthful voice couldn't be measured. She said, "I've missed you."

"And I've missed you," he said.

"How long will you be in New York?"

"About three weeks more," he told her. "But that's why I've called you. I'm coming back for overnight. I'll be leaving on a late shuttle flight this afternoon. Can I pick you up for dinner?"

"Yes, I'd like that," she agreed.

"What time?"

"Around seven," she said. "But I'd rather you didn't come here."

"Oh?" he sounded mystified.

"I'll meet you at the restaurant."

"Is anything wrong?"

195

"Not really. But I think it would be best to meet wherever we're going to eat. It will save time." She didn't want to upset him and she didn't dare tell him over the phone what had been going on.

He still sounded puzzled. "How about the Ritz Cafe? You're not far from the Ritz Carlton Hotel."

"Isn't that awfully expensive?" she worried, practical even in the face of threat.

He laughed. "Not as expensive as the dining room upstairs. And I can afford it. I've been going out at night very little here."

"My evenings have been relatively quiet too," she said with grim humor. "I'll tell you all about it when we meet."

"Seven o'clock at the Ritz. I'll wait in the lobby," he said. "If anything should delay me getting away from here I'll let you know."

"I hope nothing does," she said, her nervous state showing in her voice for the first time.

"You sound jittery," Adam said, catching the strained note at once.

"I'm fine," she hastened to say. "It's just that I'll be disappointed if you don't get back."

"And so will I," he said. "By the way I see by the newspapers your Madame Helene predicted that subway wreck."

"Yes," she said in a small voice.

"It's giving her a lot of attention," he said. "Much going on there?"

"Some reporters were here this morning," she said.

"I can imagine that," he said dryly. "Well, you

found yourself a spot where the action is, I can't deny that. But I'd like to see you away from there."

She didn't want to get into it on the phone. "I'll see you at seven," she said.

And this ended their conversation. She put the phone down with a warm feeling of hope. She could only confide so much in Adam. But his advice was bound to be helpful. And she had missed him.

She returned to her work and continued uninterrupted until Dr. Martin Gill came into her office. He was dressed for the street and he seemed to be regarding her with avid interest.

"How do you feel today?" he asked.

She played it cool. "About as usual. My headaches never seem to go these days. I'm almost getting used to them."

His hawk face showed sympathy. "I believe they will pass. You must be patient."

Diana smiled wanly. "I'll try to remember that."

"You are a Gemini," he reminded her. "I have great faith in the strength of Geminis. And I want you to know that I'm your friend. Don't think of me merely as an employer. My interest in you is too great for that."

She was at once suspicious that he had listened to her conversation with Adam on long distance. She said, "Thank you."

His burning hypnotic eyes were boring into her. "The events of yesterday prove that this organization has an exiting future. You can play an important part in it."

"I need to think about it," she told him.

"I wish you would," he said, seriously. "I'm making a special trip to the Washington Street headquarters. They say the orders for charts are coming in like mad. We're caught without nearly enough printed. I'll be back by mid-afternoon if there are any calls. I'll leave word with Miss Carlton."

She waited until he was out of the building and then she looked up the phone number of Walter Glendon's sister in Brockton. She found it and put the call through. In a moment she had Ruth Myers on the line.

"I've been reading about the accident and Madame Helene's prediction," Walter Glendon's sister said. "What does it mean?"

"It could have a significant bearing on your brother's death," Diana told her. "There is a close parallel in the cases."

"You mean this is planned evil?" There was horror in the voice of the young woman at the other end of the line.

"There is a chance. I can't promise anything yet. Though I know more than when we talked." She paused. "One thing. When you first noticed the personality change in your brother did he complain of headaches?"

"Yes, he did," the girl replied in a surprised tone. "I'd forgotten. That was at the beginning. Later he was merely sullen and withdrawn. He never mentioned how he was feeling."

"That may be helpful," Diana told her. "I'll be in touch with you later."

"Are you calling from that house on Beacon Street?"

198

"Yes."

The girl at the other end of the phone said, "I'd be careful. I'm sure there's great danger for you there."

Diana put down the phone with a solemn expression on her attractive face. Walter Glendon's sister had given her the information she'd been looking for. The young poet had complained of headaches. And she knew how he'd come by them. In the same way she had. Dr. Martin Gill had given her predecessor the same treatment of drugged incense through the air-conditioner outlet that he was giving her.

That was how he'd wrecked the young man's health and will. Left him a confused victim of a drug which had been secretly administered to him in his sleeping hours. And so she had been slated as the next victim. Well, Dr. Martin Gill could be in for a surprise.

Her curiosity about the diabolical drug grew as her realization of its danger was revealed to her. She was anxious to know exactly what it was and where it came from. As she sat there considering this it struck her that Madame Helene must know. She'd mostly avoided the old woman lately. But perhaps she might be able to extract this vital information from her.

She took the elevator up to the top floor and the apartment of the ancient astrologer. The hallway was murky when she got off the elevator. It had turned into a gray day of mixed showers and the apartment reflected the gloomy outdoor atmosphere. She moved into the big room with its stage and the chaise lounge where Madame Helene usually rested.

And the old woman was stretched out on it. Diana hurried down the length of the big room, being careful of the slippery hardwood floor. As she mounted the stage to stand by the old woman, Madame Helene opened her eyes.

"What do you want?" she asked peevishly.

Diana managed a smile for her. "To make sure that you are comfortable. The doctor has gone out."

Madame Helen's mask-like white face showed no expression but her eyes blazed angrily. Those ancient, sunken eyes. "I have Anna to take care of me. I don't need you."

"I'm only trying to be friendly," Diana said in a mild tone.

The old woman was sitting up now. "Young faces!" she said with a sneer. "Faces of deceit."

"I try to do my work well," she insisted. She was beginning to despair of reaching the old woman. Communication was especially difficult not only because of the great variance in their ages but because of the astrologer's failing mental state.

Ancient eyes peered at her from under the white folds of eyelids. "Anna doesn't trust you," she said in her quavering voice. "And Anna has a peasant's instincts about people."

"What do you think about the subway wreck?" Diana asked carefully.

The old woman raised her head and those strange eyes glared at her. "What subway wreck?"

"Then Doctor Gill didn't tell you." She'd guessed this but wanted to pretend she hadn't realized. In this desperate game you had to play a crafty hand.

"What is it that Martin should have told me?" Madame Helene demanded peevishly. "What is this about a subway wreck?"

"There was a serious one yesterday," Diana said. "And you predicted there might be one. All the papers are full of it."

The old woman's mouth gaped open. "You must be lying!"

"I can show you the papers if you like," she said.

"Why didn't they tell me?" the astrologer wailed in her old woman's voice. "Anna or Martin should have told me. They have no right to keep me in the dark!"

"The man who caused the accident was here the other night," Diana went on. "He was very unstable. And he reacted very strongly to that incense, you know what I mean."

"Agrisha!" The old woman snapped angrily. "Martin got a supply of it from Mexico a few weeks ago. It comes from India."

"Yes, I know," she said, trying to lead her on to talk more.

But Madame Helene was not to be so easily fooled. The burning eyes showed suspicion. "What do you know?" she demanded. "How could you know anything about agrisha? It is Martin's secret and mine!"

"I meant I knew just what you'd told me now," Diana said.

The old woman stood up on the shadowed stage, her long black velvet dress with its high neck, necklace of pearls and ancient hair-do with a pearl ornament on it, giving her the eerie look of one of the ghosts stepped out from those endless old movies that Martin Gill ground out for her.

201

She pointed a finger at Diana dramatically, "Get out of here! I won't have intruders on my set. I'll call the director!"

Diana was frightened to note the ancient astrologer's serious state of upset. In her angry confusion Madame Helene had slipped back into the jargon of her Hollywood days. The mad old woman presented an absurd picture of authority and dignity forever lost.

"I'm sorry," Diana apologized. "I didn't mean to bother you so." And she quickly left the stage and retreated out of the room.

From behind her on the stage came the old woman's petulant voice screaming, "Anna! Anna! Where are you, Anna?"

Diana drew a deep sigh of relief when she reached the refuge of the elevator. As it creakingly made its way down to her floor she reviewed what had been told her by the old woman. The incense was a drug called agrisha. Its source was India but Dr. Martin Gill was apparently smuggling it in illegally from Mexico.

She went back to her desk after lunch. Miss Carlton came with the mail and a message that Dr. Martin Gill would not be returning until early evening. "He's had to make a trip out to the printer in Worcester," the prim woman explained. "Something about getting an extra lot of charts out quickly."

"He was worried about that," Diana agreed.

"There's been a young woman tearing off the phone to talk to him," Miss Carlton said mournfully. "If she calls again can I let you talk to her?"

"If you like," Diana said. "I'm not sure that I'll be able to help her."

"Just so she won't be bothering me," the older woman said with a look of annoyance. "This has been an awful day."

"A lot of calls?"

"More than that," Miss Carlton said. "Everything seems to be going wrong. When you were up in your apartment at lunch time Anna was down pestering me."

Diana wasn't surprised to hear this. She knew the state Madame Helene had been in when she left her. And she'd been screaming for Anna. She pretended surprise, asking, "What about Anna?"

"That black witch!" Miss Carlton said venomously. "She wanted me to try and get in touch with Dr. Gill."

"Oh?"

"As if Dr. Gill would pay any attention to her! He'd have fired her if Madame Helene wasn't so devoted to her. She claimed the Madame wasn't feeling well and Dr. Gill should know about it."

Diana raised her brows. "Perhaps he should."

"I couldn't reach him," Miss Carlton said. "But I was worried and so I went up to the apartment to see for myself how she was. And do you know what she was doing?"

"No."

"Sitting on that chaise lounge with some kind of old scrapbook on her lap, going over it and talking to herself. I never even bothered going to her. I just came right back down. For all her predictions I know what's wrong with that old woman. She's crazy!"

Diana felt some relief at the report on Madame Helene. "As long as she isn't ill."

Miss Carlton went off in her angry mood. Diana made no real attempt to work. She had lost all interest in anything but settling accounts with the diabolical Dr. Gill and getting away from the somber old mansion forever. She was glad that Madame Helene had gotten over her upset spell and hoped the astrologer might forget all about the scene between them.

It wouldn't be long until she would be meeting Adam at the Ritz. And she was looking forward to it more every minute. The house was bearing down on her. The morning paper had reported an extra death among those injured in the subway accident and stated the authorities were investigating every angle of the wreck in an effort to account for it. Her reaction to this was grim. Unless she was able to do something she very much doubted that their investigations would ever lead them to this house on Beacon Street.

Her phone rang and when she answered it a youthful female voice said, "This is Mary Wright. I'd like to speak to Dr. Gill."

"I'm afraid he's out," she said.

"But I must get in touch with him," the girl worried.

"I don't think that's possible," Diana told her. "I seem to find your name familiar. Are you the young woman who was here last night?"

"Yes. Is that Miss Lewis?"

"Yes," Diana said. "I'm sorry but Dr. Gill is out of the city. A printing problem took him to Worcester."

"I see," the girl said, sounding relieved. "Then he probably won't be expecting me tonight."

"I'd doubt it."

"I was to come back for another lesson in hypnotism," Mary Wright said. "And I can't do it. I have to substitute here for a girl who is ill."

"I'm sure Dr. Gill will understand," Diana said. "I'll leave a note on his desk."

"Thank you," Mary Wright said. "I enjoyed last night's session so much. Dr. Gill was actually able to hypnotize me for the first time. He says I'm a fine subject. And he put everything down on a cassette recorder. But he wouldn't let me hear it."

"Interesting," Diana said, and it was to her. She wondered if he always recorded those hypnotic sessions. And whether there might be one of her being coached to carry that bomb to the labor office.

"Well, I'll call again the day after tomorrow," the girl said. "That's one of the disadvantages of being an airline hostess. You're away so much."

Diana listened in dazed disbelief. She managed, "Yes, I suppose so."

They said goodbye and she put down the phone with a stunned expression on her pretty face. An airline hostess! Of course that was why Dr. Martin Gill was so interested in her. He'd already enrolled her in the group sessions and now he was practicing hypnotism on her. In a little while, a few weeks or months at the most, there would be mention in Madame Helene's column of some coming tragedy in the air. And in the course of events, Mary Wright, under the doctor's sinister direction would make the prediction come true.

Mary Wright was being groomed for death and mass murder!

205

Diana was sickened by the thought. And she knew that now she must work more quickly than ever. And she must succeed. Otherwise this nightmare would continue and who knew how many innocent people would die?

She decided to leave her office early and went out to tell Miss Carlton so. The prim woman sniffed. "You can do what you like. I have to stay here until five. But I won't be at this desk a minute longer than that. He can go off and leave everything in a mess if he likes. But he needn't expect me to try and straighten it out."

Diana didn't wait to hear anymore. She was too concerned about what she'd discovered. She went down the dark hall to the elevator. But when she reached it she saw that it was in service. She could hear its complaining cables and then she heard it clank to a halt. The gate swung open and a wild looking Anna emerged to come menacingly towards her.

"You make trouble!" the big, swarthy woman hissed and raised a huge hand as if to slap her.

CHAPTER TWELVE

Diana stepped back quickly. She decided that the only way to deal with the enraged peasant woman was to boldly stand up to her. So with a stern expression she shot back, "I'd be careful if I were you. Dr. Gill will hear of any rash thing you may do. And you'll be answerable to him!"

The massive, swarthy-faced woman continued to stand there in a menacing fashion. But Diana could tell her words had taken some effect. Anna grated, "The doctor will also hear about you! What you have done to the Madame!"

"You needn't worry about that," Diana bluffed.

Anna went on glaring at her for a moment longer and then waddled off down the dark hall. Relief swept through Diana and she quickly got into the elevator and went up to the second floor.

She hastily changed into a smart two-piece hound's-tooth suit of black and white wool. Then she left the old house as quickly as she could. Above all else she hadn't wanted another confrontation with the venomous Anna. Her mind was still in an unhappy whirl as she headed for Arlington Street and the Ritz Hotel.

Adam was already standing in the lobby waiting for her. The sight of his familiar pleasant face gave her a moment's respite from her fear and confusion. He epitomized the proper Bostonian in his Ivy League dark suit and conservative haircut with no hint of sideburns.

He greeted her with a brief kiss. "Wonderful!" he said with a smile. "You look wonderful and you're on time!"

She laughed wryly. "I couldn't get here soon enough."

"I have our table reserved," he told her as he led her out to the Ritz Cafe.

The room was softly-lighted and they had a table for two by a window looking out on Newbury Street. They ordered and then she gave him a knowing glance.

"I don't want you to say that you told me so," she said. "But you were right about it being a mistake to take on the job with Madame Helene."

Adam looked concerned. "If you know that why have you remained there?"

"Various reasons," she said. "One being that I feel some responsibility about a discovery I've made."

"What sort of discovery?"

She hesitated. "I have reason to believe, though I can't prove it yet, that there is something criminal going on in that house."

He frowned. "Then you should get out and tell the police. It's their job not yours."

She grimaced unhappily. "The point is I haven't enough facts to present to them yet."

"The chances are you never will have," he warned

208

her. "What kind of criminal acts are you referring to?"

Diana looked at him solemnly. "It has to do with the predictions. I believe Dr. Martin Gill is deliberately setting up happenings to match the prophecies of Madame Helene."

Adam looked astounded. "You're suggesting that things like the subway wreck are being engineered by those people?"

"Not directly," she said. "But they are creating an atmosphere which makes such things possible."

He showed a puzzled light in his eyes. "I'm not sure that I follow you."

"I expected that you wouldn't," she said. "It's not all that clear yet. When I learn the whole truth I'll tell you. For the time being that's all I can say."

"You've involved me without really telling me anything," he accused her. "I don't call that fair."

She smiled wanly. "Just having you here to talk to is all I need. It helps more than you know. And I can always get in touch with you quickly if I want you."

"Don't forget I have to return to New York for another three weeks," he reminded her.

"But you'll be back here permanently then?"

"I hope so."

"The three weeks will pass quickly," she said.

He frowned. "Even knowing the little you've told me I can't allow you to go on staying at that house on Beacon Street. Resign in the morning."

"I will if I can," she promised. But unless events developed very fast she knew that wasn't likely.

Their food came and the discussion was dropped. The meal was excellent and afterward they relaxed over a liqueur. Adam again brought up the question of her staying on at Madame Helene's but she avoided the topic by suggesting they go to the Charles Playhouse on Warrendon Street for a performance of a Shaw play.

"The curtain is at eight-thirty tonight," she explained. "It's usually at seven-thirty. But on evenings when they give two performances the times are five-thirty and eight-thirty."

Adam glanced at his watch. "If you really want to see the play."

"I'd like to," she said. She actually wasn't in the mood for a play but she wanted to fill in their time together without arguments. And Adam was so unhappy about her remaining with Madame Helene's organization. The play would prevent them from endlessly going over it and keep her from getting back to that sinister old house too early.

They walked along Arlington Street past the fashionable windows and by the tall stone buildings housing banks and other financial organizations. They crossed the street at the Statler-Hilton and headed for the narrow, winding lanes of the older section of Boston where the Charles Playhouse was located. Diana tried to keep her mind off the dark business in which she was so hopelessly involved without much success.

Adam kept up a running monologue of argument against her exposing herself to more danger in the employ of the astrological publishing company. "Let someone else expose them," he said. "Why should it depend on you?"

"Please, Adam," she said, "I'd rather not talk about

it anymore now." They headed along Warrendon Street with its shabby red brick buildings and the marquee of the Charles Playhouse blazed out in the darkness ahead of them.

Adam bought tickets at the door and they went upstairs to the intimate theatre-in-the-round. Fortunately the curtain rose a few minutes later and so there was no further argument between them. The play and cast were excellent but Diana was much too nervous to keep her mind on the stage. At intermission she stayed strictly with a discussion of the play as they moved around the small lobby studying various art posters that were on display.

The play ended shortly before eleven. They walked out to a main street and Adam hailed a taxi. In the privacy of the shadowed rear seat of the cab he put his arm around her and kissed her. Then he held her close. Diana enjoyed the brief interlude of happiness, but the knowledge that she was returning to Beacon Street and a possible confrontation with Dr. Martin Gill shadowed the blissful moment.

Adam stood on the steps of the tall red brick house, reluctant to leave her. "Why not let me take you back to your place in Brookline?" he asked.

"Not yet," she said. "Trust me."

"I do," he told her with concern on his pleasant face. "But I can't tell about those people in there." In the end she won. He kissed her goodnight and left in the cab.

Diana knew that she wasn't as brave as she'd pretended to be the moment she found herself alone. She watched the red taillights of the taxi with Adam in it vanish in the night traffic of Beacon Street and her heart began to pound in an erratic, nervous fashion. Fumbling with her key she let herself into the dark, silent hallway.

She walked quietly down towards the back of the house and the elevator. Ahead she saw light from the open doorway of Dr. Martin Gill's room and she guessed that he had returned and was in there. If she were lucky, she would get past the door without his seeing her.

Her fear increased as she neared the doorway. She'd almost gotten by when he appeared carrying a metal safe deposit box in his hands. He had apparently been in the large step-in vault at the far end of his room and had come out just in time to see her.

His hawk face at once took on an annoyed look. "Where have you been?" he demanded, coming out to the hall and blocking her way.

She swallowed hard. "I went out to dinner and the theatre. Why?"

The suave doctor continued to stare at her with those hypnotic eyes. "I can't imagine you taking off for a carefree evening after upsetting the Madame so."

"In what way?" She was again bluffing and stalling for time.

He looked grave. "Telling her about the subway accident. I think I made it clear she wasn't to be told."

"I don't remember," she said.

"I think you do," he insisted coldly. "Anna says you went up there and nagged Madame Helene into hysterics. I expected more of you. I have had such great hopes for you."

212

"It didn't occur to me it was that important," she said.

Dr. Martin Gill sighed. "You're asking me to believe that?"

"Yes."

He said, "We're on the eve of our biggest expansion. It would be a disaster to have anything happen to the Madame now."

Diana was relieved of the necessity of making a reply for at that moment there came the sound of heavy, running footsteps and breathless panting from around the corner in the other hallway. And in the next instant Anna burst out from the shadows of the corridor and approached Dr. Martin Gill.

"The Madame!" the swarthy woman gasped, paying no attention to Diana. "She's very bad! I think she's dying!" And she hurried back towards the elevator.

Consternation showed on the doctor's hawk face. He wavered for a moment and then ran back into his office and Diana heard the click of the heavy vault door as he hurled it closed. Then he came out and followed after Anna.

It had all happened so quickly that it took a moment for Diana to realize what was going on. Madame Helene had suffered another seizure and perhaps a fatal one. She felt a slight stab of self-reproach knowing she had no doubt badly upset the confused old woman. But this passed with the following thought that she had done it to try and halt the sinister doctor in his campaign of horror.

The house was deathly silent again with the other two on the upper floor ministering to the stricken woman. Slowly she entered the office and stood for a moment staring at those rows of smiling faces of the dead Hollywood greats? Was Madame Helene at this moment about to join them? To become one of the wraiths who lived only in the flickering shadows of the screen?

Diana turned from staring at the photos to a study of the vault. And a thrill of excitement shot through her! The door didn't look just right to her. As if it weren't properly closed! She rushed forward and tried its handle and the door swung open easily. In his need to get away the wily Dr. Martin Gill had for once neglected to make sure the door had clicked in place properly as he normally would have done.

Her excitement grew as she looked into the interior of the vault and saw that the bulb of the drop-light was burning just as the wily doctor had left it. Slowly she stepped inside the steel-walled closet and turned her attention to the several metal filing cabinets in there. One of the drawers was open.

Tensely she began to examine its contents. There were some ledgers that she paid no attention to but laid aside. Under them was what looked to be a large and ancient scrapbook. She took this from the file and opened it at random. What she saw made her eyes open wide!

It was a picture of a smiling Dr. Martin Gill. But a likeness taken years ago when he was a young man. Above the photo was a heavy black headline: "FAKE HOLLYWOOD MEDICO." And underneath in type only a little smaller was the summary of the long story that followed.

She scanned it tensely, reading: "Fake Hollywood youth doctor exposed! Gland treatments proven hoax! Doctor's credentials shown false! Former hospital orderly given prison sentence!"

Diana read feverishly, enough to know all she needed to about the crafty Dr. Martin Gill. As she'd begun to suspect he was not a doctor at all. He was a confidence man with a prison record. But why had Madame Helene allowed such a person to gain control of her and her organization? Blame it on age and failing health! Perhaps.

She frantically turned the pages of the scrapbook. Some of the items collected by the fake doctor showed him in smiling photos with many of the stars whose likenesses appeared on his office wall. There he was standing by them in the days of his glory. The stars were invariably gazing at him with admiration. Why shouldn't they have worshipped him? After all, he was selling them youth. The thing they prized above all else. And now they were dust in their graves and faded smiling faces on his office wall. But his sinister career went on!

There were several blank pages in the album next. The pages were yellowed with age and had a musty smell. And then she came to another section of clippings. This time she gasped aloud. Under a full page heading: "FILM STAR ACCUSED OF MURDER" was a striking photo of a young and lovely Madame Helene!

But the name of the star was Pearl Williams! Diana raced through the account aware that Martin Gill could return at any moment. The news story mentioned Pearl Williams as being one of the most promising of younger stars. The year was 1922. Pearl Williams had been charged and tried for killing her lover, a famous director of the period. But the gun used in the murder hadn't been found and no witnesses had turned up. As a result Pearl Williams had been acquitted. But the story went on to say that she was still under a shadow and the studio had broken their contract with her. They pointed out she was thirty-four years old and it was likely her career was at an end.

Staring at the pasted account in the scrapbook Diana did some quick mental arithmetic and came to the conclusion that this made the former screen star eighty-four. Madame Helene was a long way from being over the century mark as Martin Gill had insisted. This had been a ruse to throw people off the track of the true identity of the ancient astrologer.

It was easy to guess how the film star with a wrecked career and the fake doctor had come together in this unholy alliance. They would have known each other in Hollywood. And the wily Gill would have devised the scheme of operating an astrological service. Using Pearl Williams as the mysterious Madame Helene he had built it to fantastic success. But greed for power and money had no doubt taken over. And so Gill had resorted to murder to reach for greater power and more money. She hastily put the scrapbook back in the file and noticed the cassette tape recorder on the top of another filing cabinet. She was reaching for it when she heard the approaching footsteps in the hall.

Terrified she quickly stepped out of the vault, but not soon enough. The wily Dr. Martin Gill had entered the office in time to catch her. His hawk face was a strange study of mixed consternation and despair.

His first words surprised her. In a dull voice, he said, "She's dead! She died in my arms!"

Diana swallowed hard. Wondering what his next reaction would be. She said, "I'm sorry."

Now it seemed full awareness belatedly came to him. He stared at her weirdly. "How did you get in there?"

"You left the door open by accident," she faltered. "I went in to turn off the light and close the door."

"You're lying," he snapped, the old knife-keen Martin Gill again. He pointed a thin accusing finger at her. "You were in there spying while Madame Helene was breathing her last."

Diana knew it was time to take a stand. Meeting his gaze directly, she said, "Pearl Williams."

He faced her tensely. And now he took a deep breath. "So you know!"

"All about her and about you, Dr. Gill," she stressed the doctor with sarcasm.

"That's lost in the past," he said rather breathlessly. "It doesn't matter!"

"Maybe not," she said. "But the deaths you're causing now do. I know what you've been up to making sure your predictions would come true. I know you caused Walter Glendon and Julia James to die. And the operator of the subway train and those who were killed in the wreck. Your latest victim is to be that blonde Mary Wright. You're twisting her mind with hypnotism just as you've tried to twist mine with that incense! Filtering it into my room in the night!"

"Crazy talk!" he told her harshly. "No one will believe you. You can't prove any of it!"

"I think I can," she said with more confidence than she felt.

The hawk-faced Gill took a step closer to her. "No, Diana," he said pleadingly. "Don't think that way. You and I can make a wonderful team. You can be the new Madame Helene. I've been grooming you for it from the first!"

"No!"

"Listen to me," he said eagerly. "I can make you wealthy beyond your dreams and famous. I picked you because you had the same birth sign as Pearl and you were lovely. I've been selling you to the others as her heir. We don't have to rely on the predictions anymore. I promise you I'll play it straight if you'll join with me."

Diana stared at him in disbelief. "You have to be joking!"

He shook his head. "I'm an old man but I'm healthy and strong. And I'm in love with you. You must have guessed that! I can make you happy and bring you more money than you'll ever need. I never loved Pearl. I only pretended to because I needed her. But it's different with you. I swear I love you, Diana!"

She listened to his impassioned pleading in stunned dismay. But his final words were lost to her. For now she was staring at the doorway and an expression of horror crossed her face. She was staring at a ghost! The ghost of the dead Pearl Williams was standing there in the shadows with a gun in her hand. The gun

218

was pointed at Dr. Martin Gill and her sunken, burning eyes were fixed on him with ineffable hatred.

"Martin!" she spoke his name in her quavering, aged voice.

It was the fake doctor's turn to register incredulity and then terror. He gazed over his shoulder at the apparition in the shadowed doorway and uttered a pitiful, "No!"

And then the gun in the phantom's hand blazed and Martin Gill's look of terror turned to one of blankness as he fell down in a crumpled heap. Diana cried out and waited for the gun to be turned on her. But the figure in the doorway had vanished as suddenly as it had appeared. Diana stared down at the motionless figure of Martin Gill and the spreading pool of blood around him. And she screamed again!

But there was no escaping from the nightmare. Somehow she got sufficient control of herself to stumble across to his desk and put through a frantic call to the police. Then she knelt down by the fake doctor and could detect no sign of a heartbeat. She was beyond thinking clearly.

And she was still in a daze when the sirens sounded outside the house and the police rang the doorbell. She groped her way along the dark hall and let them in.

A thick-set man in plain clothes was the first to question her. "What's happened?" he asked.

"Someone's been shot," she managed in a strained voice. "Shot by a ghost!" And she collapsed.

She was stretched out on a sofa and the thick-set man was standing over her. "Feeling better?" he asked, as she opened her eyes.

"Yes," she said in a near whisper.

"You were right," the man in plain clothes said grimly. "Dr. Martin Gill is dead. But we haven't found the gun or your ghost."

She stared at him. "What about Madame Helene?"

"Dead. Died of a heart attack upstairs," the man said. "There's a servant with her, name of Anna Martinelli."

"I know," she said. "It was the ghost of Madame Helene who had the gun. She killed him."

The man in plain clothes looked skeptical. "I think we're getting things mixed up a little. Likely the old woman came down here and shot him and then went upstairs and died from the excitement."

She raised herself up on an elbow. "But he said she had died before he came downstairs."

The detective studied her with a grim expression on his broad face. "You'd better hope that he was wrong. Otherwise you can find yourself on the suspect list."

That night they took her back to her Brookline apartment. She called Adam in New York and he promised to fly back the next morning. Then she took a tablet given her by the police doctor and sank into a drugged sleep. In the gray morning that followed she felt groggy but rested.

The grisly events of the night before still were terrifyingly vivid to her. Things had happened so swiftly she'd barely been able to keep up with them. She'd not tried to tell the police any of the horror that lay behind the death and murder. With Madame Helene and Martin Gill both dead, no purpose could be served by dragging all the sinister events into the open. And unless there were some strong evidence on the tape in that cassette recorder she'd seen in the vault she doubted if she'd ever be able to prove her accusations.

Martin Gill had been far too crafty to leave my record of his evil maneuverings. It was more or less a closed book. But one thing had to be cleared up. The police would have to uncover definite proof as to who the murderer had been. The confusion of time concerning Madame Helene's death, or Pearl Williams', to use her correct name, made it seem that the fatal shot must have been fired by a phantom. And the Boston police rarely accepted ghostly explanations for killings. So she was under suspicion.

She'd been given strict instructions not to leave her apartment. And when Adam arrived at Logan Airport he took a taxi from there to her place. After the embrace and kisses of reunion had been taken care of he began to ask some pertinent questions.

"What's been bothering me is you. Are you in the clear?"

"I hope so," she said.

"But you're not sure."

The thick-set man in plain clothes came to the apartment while Adam was still there. She introduced him to the detective who had the good Irish name of Kelly.

Detective Kelly eyed Adam and said, "This young lady is your fiancée?"

Adam nodded and smiled at Diana who sat in an easy chair near him. "She is going to be."

The thick-set man looked interested. "Why did you allow her to work in a place like that? There were too many mixed-up people in that house on Beacon Street."

"I did it against his wishes," she spoke up quickly.

Adam frowned. "I should have taken a firmer stand with her. I realize that now."

"I guess so," Detective Kelly said, taking a notebook from his inside jacket pocket. "Her employers were both living under assumed names. And both of them had been in trouble with the police in the past. When did you learn Madame Helene was really Pearl Williams?" he turned to Diana on this question.

"Just a few minutes before the shooting," she said.

Detective Kelly stared at her. "And you still maintain that it was Pearl Williams you saw with the gun?"

"Or her ghost," she said.

"Or her ghost," the Detective repeated in a wry tone. "According to your own evidence this Martin Gill told you Pearl Williams was already dead when he came downstairs."

"Yes."

The thick-set man consulted his notebook. "Now the servant, Anna, also states that her employer died in Martin Gill's arms before he went down in the elevator."

There was a silence in the room. Then Adam spoke up, "Obviously there was some mistake. The old woman must have fired the shot that killed Martin Gill after he thought she'd died. Then she found her way back up in the elevator and really died."

The Detective lifted his eyebrows. "What about the maid's version?"

"She could also be wrong," Adam insisted. "She

probably thought as Martin Gill did that her mistress was dead. Perhaps she left the body for a little. And Madame Helene regained consciousness and went downstairs while this Anna was absent. Then came back to approximately the same spot and died."

The Detective nodded. "That's fairly smart thinking, Mister. It's just the way we've reconstructed the case. And probably how it will go down in the books."

A vague feeling of uneasiness was bothering Diana. She gave both men a serious look. "I don't know," she said. "Martin Gill always insisted there was something supernatural about the old woman. After last night I confess I think the same way."

Detective Kelly smiled bleakly. "It's interesting you should say that, Miss Lewis. When we found out the old woman was Pearl Williams we called for information on that other murder case she was mixed up with in Hollywood. Eeveryone felt she was guilty but she got off chiefly because the murder weapon was never found."

"I know," Diana said.

"But of course they had the bullet," Detective Kelly went on. "And we had them transmit a detailed photo of it." He paused significantly. "The markings on the bullet exactly matched the markings on the bullet we found in Martin Gill last night."

Diana stared at him, a shadow of fear on her face. "And you haven't been able to locate the gun yet?"

"No. It was the same weapon that was used in that long ago murder. He closed his notebook. "Somehow I have an idea that gun will never be found."

Adam was standing by the chair in which Diana sat.

He put a hand on her shoulder and she gave him a look of understanding. Then she stared off into space with a hint of fear in her lovely eyes. She was picturing the big dark room in Madame Helene's apartment. Up on the screen wraith-like figures acted out some forgotten drama, only the drone of the projector broke the silence. Suddenly the face of Pearl Williams showed for just a moment to gaze sadly at her from the screen, then mingle with those other ghosts and vanish.